*"I'd like t..........
as the playful arm wrestling match e.......
his eyes were only for Morgan . . .*

She caught her breath, her heart suddenly thudding out of control, her body beginning to tremble. "Cole," she whispered. Beyond that single word she couldn't speak. She was hypnotized by the determined, sensual expression in his dark eyes, his intriguing half smile, the electricity emanating from him.

"Let's make this contest more interesting," Cole suggested. "What do I get if I win?"

Morgan had begun to regain her poise, and remembered the steely strength of Cole's arms. She knew she would lose this match. "You name the stakes," she said with a tiny smile.

"All right," Cole said quietly. "You leave here with me—and only me—when the match is over."

Morgan felt dizzy, thrilled at his words and what they promised. "You're on." She put her elbow on the table and clasped Cole's hand. A blazing heat surged through her when his long fingers meshed with hers. As she felt his strength, she knew that even at her best she'd be no match for him; with her insides softening and her limbs melting, she didn't have a chance against him, in arm wrestling or anything else. . . .

WHAT ARE *LOVESWEPT* ROMANCES?

They are stories of true romance and touching emotion. We believe those two very important ingredients are constants in our highly sensual and very believable stories in the *LOVESWEPT* line. Our goal is to give you, the reader, stories of consistently high quality that may sometimes make you laugh, sometimes make you cry, but are always fresh and creative and contain many delightful surprises within their pages.

Most romance fans read an enormous number of books. Those they truly love, they keep. Others may be traded with friends and soon forgotten. We hope that each *LOVESWEPT* romance will be a treasure—a "keeper." We will always try to publish

LOVE STORIES YOU'LL NEVER FORGET
BY AUTHORS YOU'LL ALWAYS REMEMBER

The Editors

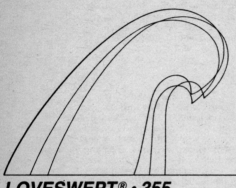

LOVESWEPT® • 355

Gail Douglas
The Dreamweavers:
Swashbuckling Lady

 BANTAM BOOKS
NEW YORK • TORONTO • LONDON • SYDNEY • AUCKLAND

SWASHBUCKLING LADY

A Bantam Book / October 1989

LOVESWEPT® *and the wave device are registered
trademarks of Bantam Books, a division of
Bantam Doubleday Dell Publishing Group, Inc.
Registered in U.S. Patent
and Trademark Office and elsewhere.*

*If you would be interested in receiving protective vinyl
covers for your Loveswept books, please write to this address
for information:*

Loveswept
Bantam Books
P.O. Box 985
Hicksville, NY 11802

ISBN 0-553-22037-3

Published simultaneously in the United States and Canada

---

*Bantam Books are published by Bantam Books, a division
of Bantam Doubleday Dell Publishing Group, Inc. Its trademark, consisting of the words "Bantam Books" and the
portrayal of a rooster, is Registered in U.S. Patent and
Trademark Office and in other countries. Marca Registrada.
Bantam Books, 666 Fifth Avenue, New York, New York 10103.*

PRINTED IN THE UNITED STATES OF AMERICA

O   0 9 8 7 6 5 4 3 2 1

To my mother,
who taught me
the strength of femininity
and the
femininity of strength.

One

Cole Jameson felt as if he'd slipped through a time warp.

In the eerie silence that had settled over his crippled boat, it was easy to imagine that the brigantine slicing through the glassy waters toward him, its skull and crossbones boldly flapping in the breeze, was an eighteenth-century pirate vessel on the attack. For just an instant the hairs rose on the back of his neck, as much from sudden excitement as from the gentle Gulf breeze.

Then he laughed at his momentary lapse, realizing that the approaching ship was just another Key West tourist gimmick.

Tipping back his battered canvas fedora and lowering his sunglasses to peer over their rim, Cole silently thanked the brig's captain for coming to his rescue, unlike the skippers of several other passing vessels who had ignored his efforts to flag them down—efforts that, he had to concede, had been halfhearted. He found the whole situation humiliating. The one thing he hated about learning something was the knew-nothing stage—and he definitely knew precious little about his new boat.

As the ship bore down on his cabin cruiser, Cole was able to make out the ornate gilt letters on its polished black hull. His seagoing Samaritan was the *Anne of the Indies*. Obviously whoever had named the ship had seen plenty of pirate movies on late-night television. As the craft drew closer he could hear *Captain Blood* music over the deep throb of the diesel engines.

The *Anne* also had a full passenger load of curious tourists. Muttering a soft oath, Cole was mildly irritated that his ineptness as a sailor would be witnessed so publicly.

But he reminded himself to be grateful. Now he wouldn't have to radio for help or, if none came, spend the night drifting aimlessly less than a mile from the Key West marina where he'd arranged for a berth for his proud new purchase.

As the brigantine drew alongside, a wiry crew member shinnied up one of the masts. The pseudo-pirate held on with one hand and cupped the other around his mouth. "Ya got trouble, mister?" he shouted, sounding more like a Bronx street urchin than an exotic buccaneer.

"The engine quit on me," Cole called back, removing his sunglasses and slipping them into the pocket of his knit polo shirt. "I'm not sure what's wrong."

"I wouldn't know either," the younger man said cheerfully. "I'm only an acrobat. Hang on while I ask the expert."

"*You* hang on!" Cole said with a grin, amused but genuinely concerned. "It looks pretty risky up there."

As his gaze swept over the brigantine Cole decided that the operators of this particular tourist attraction had a fine eye for detail. The ship seemed to glow with pride, its gilt trim gleaming in the sunlight, its lines as smoothly curved as a woman's body, its figurehead of a boldly sensual, dark-haired, and sloe-eyed beauty sculpted and painted by a master hand. Judging by the deckhands Cole could see, they all played their piratical roles to the hilt, swaggering and strutting in full costume to the obvious delight of the passengers.

The acrobat hanging from the mast cupped his hand around his mouth again. "The cap'n says the best plan is for you to hitch your boat to us and come aboard. We'll throw you some lines and a rope ladder. One of our guys will climb down and give you a hand."

Cole was impressed by the efficiency of his helpers. Clearly the *Anne of the Indies* crew members were more than showmen. They were sailors who knew what they were doing—unlike himself, he thought with annoyance.

It seemed only minutes before his little cruiser was secured firmly to the brig and he was climbing up the rope ladder toward the deck of the *Anne*, preparing a small thank-you speech for the ship's captain.

On deck he gathered his dignity despite all the curious and amused gazes fastened on him. He hated being singled out. He also hated being seen as less than competent. Above all, he hated needing help from anyone. "Where's your captain?" he asked the pirate who'd scampered down from the mast. "I'd like to pay my respects and offer my thanks."

"Right this way," the young man said with a theatrical sweep of his arm toward the opposite side of the deck.

Cole took one step, then stopped dead, his heart slamming against the wall of his chest. "*She's* the captain of this ship?" he asked in a low, tight voice, gaping at the skipper.

"She sure is," came the cheerful answer. "That's Cap'n Morgan herself."

Pummeled by sudden, conflicting emotions, Cole couldn't move. *Cap'n Morgan,* he repeated silently. The mischievous angel who'd been at the fringes of his consciousness and inhabiting too many of his dreams for the past few weeks was standing with one arm leaning on the rail of the ship, staring back at him, looking as shocked as he felt.

He'd seen her around Key West, usually in one of the many watering holes along Duval Street, always surrounded by an odd mixture of friends, from vacationing college types to aging hippies, from well-heeled tourists to local bums, from bikers to fishermen. Her loveliness and easy laughter seemed to draw people to her like bees to a sweetly scented bloom, and Cole had found it increasingly difficult to resist her allure.

When he'd left Key West two weeks earlier to pick up his boat in Miami, he'd expected to come back and find the town duller but safer because the tall, golden-skinned woman would be gone. She was a visitor, he'd told himself. A pretty girl soaking up sun and atmosphere during her vacation. All he'd had to do was fight his attraction to her until he'd left for Miami—or so he'd thought. He hadn't counted on the way she would continue to invade his imagination even when he wasn't around her. And he certainly hadn't banked on seeing her in town when he returned.

He blinked, as if to be sure his eyes weren't playing tricks on him.

They weren't. Captain Morgan, skipper of this modern-day pirate brigantine, rescuer of stranded, amateur sailors, disturber of a man's hard-won peace, was standing right in front of him in a gauzy, flounced red skirt, waist-cinching belt, and peasant-style white blouse. She was gazing back at him, her tawny eyes flickering with emotions he couldn't read, her full, tempting mouth slightly curved in the bemused little smile she'd given him on several occasions, her strawberry blond curls framing her even features like an aureole of spun sunlight.

Cole took off his hat and raked his fingers through his hair, moving slowly toward the lovely vision, trying to collect his wits.

Morgan Sinclair felt as if she were being buffeted by high winds, though the sea within the seven-mile reef around Key West was calm.

Never in her twenty-eight years had she experienced the feelings this man could arouse in her with nothing more than a look. His eyes, as black as a tropical ocean on a moonless night, drew her into their depths until she felt as if she were caught in the vortex of a whirlpool.

For the first weeks after her arrival she'd seen the dark, quiet man often, and though she'd tried to deny the disturbing effects he'd had on her, she hadn't been able to stop thinking about him even after he'd disappeared, leaving her with the impression that he'd been a tourist who'd returned to his real life after a month in the sun.

He looked like someone who'd spent a lot longer than a month in the sun, though. Morgan was fascinated by the color of his skin, a deep, burnished copper that seemed only partly the result of a tan. She was intrigued by the silkiness of his black hair, and his aquiline features, invariably dusted by a five-o'clock shadow, had carved themselves in sharp relief into her memory.

All at once Morgan realized that her crew and passengers were watching the encounter with interest, and she was embarrassed, wondering how much of her unprecedented attraction to this man was showing. "Hi," she managed to say softly. "Welcome aboard the *Anne of the Indies*." She signaled silently to the first mate to get the brig under way again.

Cole cleared his throat. "Thank you, Captain." He thrust out his hand to grasp hers. "I'm Cole Jameson, and I appreciate the rescue. Even the coast guard and the police patrol boats were ignoring me."

"Didn't you radio for help?"

"I was about to admit defeat and do just that when your brig came along," Cole answered, thinking he'd have preferred to stay adrift than to have this particular lady be the one to pick him up. Learning that she was in fact the captain of an impressive sailing vessel and its finely tuned crew had sharpened his feeling of inadequacy. He didn't like the feeling at all. But there was no sense trying to pretend he was something he wasn't. "I'm not much of a sailor," he said, then couldn't help adding, "yet."

"What happened to your boat?" Morgan asked, wondering if he could hear the breathlessness in her voice. For all the acute awareness she'd felt toward this man, for all the penetrating looks they'd exchanged during the weeks before he'd disappeared from Key West, they hadn't spoken a word to each other. A startling surge of excitement coursed through her from where their hands were joined, generating such heat, she was sure Cole had felt it. Or was he its source?

Morgan was thoroughly confused.

Cole realized belatedly that he hadn't released her hand. Letting go and resting his arm on the railing, he searched his memory for the question he was sure she'd asked. Finally recalling it, he rolled his eyes in exaggerated disgust and shrugged. "The engine just conked out. A broken fuel line, I suspect."

Morgan nodded. "That's what it sounds like. It's maddening when that happens, isn't it?"

"It's especially maddening because I just bought

the thing," Cole said, somewhat comforted by her matter-of-fact remark. She made the situation sound like a common one. He grinned. "It's a secondhand cruiser—I'm afraid I might have gotten myself a lemon."

Morgan was glad her helmsman and crew were past the point of needing much guidance from her to get under way again and complete the day's journey. In her suddenly addled state she could cause a shipwreck, she thought with amazement. Why should one man, however attractive he might be, have such a devastating effect on her senses? "It's a nice-looking little craft," she said, just to fill the silence. "Did you buy it through a broker?"

"A reputable one, supposedly," Cole answered. "I picked it up in Miami. My experience with boats is limited, I'm afraid."

Morgan raised her brow in surprise. "You've come down from Miami in an unfamiliar cruiser and you say you're inexperienced? According to all the reports I've been hearing, the Atlantic has been very rough. I'd say you must be a natural sailor to come through that trip with nothing worse than fuel-line trouble."

Cole studied her as she spoke, wondering if she was pandering to his overly sensitive male ego. He hoped not. He'd experienced enough empty flattery from women to last him a lifetime. But somehow he sensed that Captain Morgan was too straightforward to bother with such games. He believed she meant what she said, and his spirits rose.

A new thought struck him. "Do you have a real name, or do you stick with the pseudonym?"

She smiled. "Morgan is my real name. Morgan Sinclair."

"Pretty coincidental," Cole murmured.

"It isn't a coincidence at all," Morgan said. "The name actually spawned the idea. A few years ago I took a course in sailing tall ships, and everyone started teasing me with that Cap'n Morgan business. The nickname stuck when I opened my own sailing school in New Orleans, and one day it hit me that day trips with a pirate crew would be a logical extension of the school. The cruises also mesh perfectly with the business I'm involved in with my sisters." Morgan frowned as she realized she was chattering nervously. As a rule, she wasn't the nervous type.

Cole's lips curved in a smile. Morgan's explanation, casually tossed off, fascinated him. What kind of business was she involved in with her sisters? How many sisters? Did they look like Morgan? If so, they couldn't be in Key West, he realized, or he'd have spotted them. Perhaps they were in New Orleans. Perhaps the Big Easy was Morgan's hometown. He couldn't place her accent, though. She didn't sound Southern, yet there was a hint of a drawl in her wonderfully low, melodious tones.

It occurred to Cole that he hadn't been so curious about anyone in a very long time.

It was another warning signal, he told himself.

Before he could decide whether to try to satisfy his curiosity on even one point, they were interrupted.

"The cruise has been wonderful," a husky female voice said.

Morgan smiled at the slim, silver-haired woman who had walked up to them. "Thank you, Mrs. Piersall. I hope your grandson enjoyed it." She grinned at a boy of about nine who was gazing up at her in adoration.

"Bobby has had a wonderful time," the woman answered. "And please call me Lydia." She reached into her purse, pulled out a business card, and handed it to Morgan. "I have a feeling we'll be doing a lot of business together. You see, I run a rather large chain of travel agencies. I'd read some items in the trades about the firm you and your sisters run, and I did a bit of research on your operation before I decided to give Bobby a treat and take your pirate cruise to check it out for myself. I'm impressed, Morgan. Most impressed. Not only will you be hearing from me, but if the other branches of Dreamweavers are as well run as this one, I'll want to get literature on all of them."

Morgan's smile widened, her face lighting up with such delight, it brought a strange ache to Cole's throat.

"You've made my day, Lydia," Morgan said. "I'll call Stefanie in New Orleans tonight and tell her the good news. She'll put you on our mailing list."

Lydia turned to Cole. "Stefanie is Morgan's older sister and president of Dreamweavers, Inc.," she explained with a touch of smugness that told Cole she was the kind of person who liked being in the know. "There are four lovely Sinclair sisters," Lydia went on, as if she'd been appointed to explain the company's operation to him. "They grew up like seagoing gypsies, roaming the world on a sailboat called *The Dreamweaver* with their adventurous parents."

Lydia paused to favor Cole with a wink. "Each sister runs a separate branch of the company in a different part of the world—Captain Morgan is the only pirate among them, however. These ladies have made a blazing success of—"

"Lydia, you're embarrassing me!" Morgan broke in, managing a good-natured smile though her cheeks were flaming.

The older woman merely laughed. "I've noticed that Morgan's good at putting the spotlight on other people, but she doesn't care much for it herself. Only in her role as a pirate does she let herself shine a little. But what a pirate she *is*, wouldn't you agree, Mr. . . . ?"

"I'm Cole Jameson," he supplied, taking her hand as she extended it.

"And what do you do, Cole?" Lydia asked.

He suppressed a frown. When he'd come to live in Key West, he'd hoped never to hear that question again. For some reason, being defined by a career had started grating on his nerves, even back home when he'd been living as if his work were all that mattered. It wasn't as if he'd turned into a well-off bum, spending his days in the sun and his nights in the bars. And he didn't have anything to hide—except, of course, the project he'd gotten involved in on a tiny island in the Gulf. The secrecy needed in that particular circumstance was temporary and for a valid reason.

But the fatuous cocktail-party query "And what

do you do?" had always bugged him. He wanted to answer that he was a man, not a job.

Good manners, however, demanded he give Lydia, who was simply being friendly, a proper response. He hadn't been able to leave his drawing-room manners behind along with everything else he'd walked away from.

His hesitation made Lydia forge ahead. "Do you live in Key West?" she asked.

"For just under a year," he replied pleasantly, realizing that Lydia, like most people, wasn't asking for answers. She just couldn't abide silence. Now *this* lady would be great at cocktail parties, he mused.

Morgan, on the other hand, wouldn't. She seemed to have little to say for herself, which surprised Cole. When she was with her pals in the casual atmosphere of the Duval Street night spots, she seemed confident and outgoing.

"Where are you from originally, Cole?" Lydia prodded.

"Philadelphia," he answered absently.

Lydia nodded. "I suppose you gravitated toward the sun," she said as she looked him over.

Cole found himself watching Morgan, barely hearing Lydia as she went on to relate how she'd started her business with one tiny hole-in-the-wall office in a small town . . .

Cole would have found the woman's constant chatter excruciating under normal circumstances, but at the moment he appreciated it. Lydia was giving him a chance to enjoy being close to Morgan without having to make small talk. He hated small talk. It was a meaningless social grace he'd hoped to abandon when he'd left Philadelphia. He liked the fact that Morgan didn't seem given to it either. In fact, the beautiful captain appeared to have drifted into a little world of her own.

He settled back to savor his first chance to gaze freely at her.

The comments Lydia had made earlier about Morgan's colorful life intrigued him. He supposed he could, like the older woman, do some research and read up on the Sinclair sisters in back issues of travel magazines. But he didn't want to learn about Morgan in a library. He wanted to make his explorations in person.

Cole felt a shaft of desire shoot through him. He wondered if the ship had a captain's cabin, the kind where Errol Flynn and Burt Lancaster had seduced their captive ladies. The thought of lifting Morgan in his arms—never mind that *she* was the captain and *he* the captive—and carrying her down there to make love to her without delay gave him something akin to a deep, pulsating pain.

Uncomfortably aware of Cole's frank scrutiny, Morgan tried unsuccessfully to concentrate on what Lydia was saying. Though she didn't want to dwell on her inexplicable feelings for Cole Jameson, Morgan couldn't help herself. Something about him had intrigued her from the moment she'd spied him sitting alone at the bar where she'd gone to join some friends. Cole had been nursing a Mexican beer. He always drank Mexican beer, she'd noticed on subsequent occasions, the kind that was served with a lime wedge stuck into the neck of the bottle.

He would walk into a dimly lit room, and Morgan would spot him instantly, as if she'd been watching for him. He would perch on a stool, speak pleasantly but briefly to the bartender, drink two bottles of beer—never more than two—and leave.

Morgan didn't know why she was so drawn to him. He was good-looking in a forbidding way, but she'd met plenty of handsome characters in her life, and none of them had made strange things happen in the pit of her stomach the way he did.

Admittedly, she thought, the man would arouse any healthy woman's interest. His taut body had an animal grace about it that heated Morgan's blood. When he strode across a room, the hard sinews of his flanks rippled under the faded denim that sheathed them, the muscles of his back and arms flexed against his shirt. Morgan had found herself imagining the man hunting for prey. She'd found herself wishing *she* were that prey.

No matter how hard she'd tried not to stare, her glance had settled on him again and again, her rapt attention captured by a coil of black hair revealed at the open neck of his shirt, or by the sheer breadth of his shoulders, or by the imposing wall of his chest.

His features and coloring fascinated Morgan. His hair wasn't just dark but jet black, his eyes onyx and impenetrable, his skin deeply bronzed. Even his perpetual five-o'clock shadow snagged Morgan's imagination. She kept lapsing into daydreams of rubbing her cheek, kittenlike, against the stubble of whiskers.

He wore a disreputable canvas fedora, but always took it off indoors and placed it on the barstool beside him with all the care a Regency dandy would lavish on his silk top hat. Then, with a gesture Morgan found oddly endearing, he invariably raked his fingers through his tousled hair.

More than once the man had caught Morgan staring at him. And the smoldering expression in his dark eyes when his gaze had met hers had triggered dreams like none she'd had before.

Morgan wondered why he had never approached her. He hadn't done a thing to close the gap between them. And she'd been afflicted with an uncharacteristic, paralyzing shyness, so she hadn't tried to speak to him either.

Then he'd disappeared, and she'd never even learned his name.

Distracted by a little boy who was tearing around the deck, overly excited and obviously beyond his parents' control, Morgan motioned to one of her crew to slow him down.

The crew member, a petite, pretty redhead in knee-length cutoffs, billowing shirt, and jaunty head scarf, nodded and took three small balls from her pocket, then hunkered down in front of the child and launched into an impromptu juggling act. The boy practically skidded to a stop, watching with huge, dark eyes.

Cole, noticing the whole pantomime, chuckled quietly. "Nicely done," he said to Morgan.

She glowed as if she'd just won a coveted award.

"You know, you're absolutely marvelous with children," Lydia said. "I can't help being curious . . ." Her voice trailed off as she obviously realized that she had no business asking Morgan why she wasn't married and raising a family of her own.

Morgan merely smiled. She was used to having people wonder why she hadn't achieved wedded bliss yet. But she didn't encourage Lydia's curiosity. Gracefully she changed the subject. "Are you and Bobby staying in Key West until the end of the week?" she asked.

Nicely done again, Cole thought. His admiration for Morgan went up another notch.

He was sorry when the brig smoothly pulled up to its dock, though he knew he should be glad to escape Morgan Sinclair's spell. The kind of intense feelings she aroused in him were forbidden. There was no place for a woman in his life. Not a special woman anyway.

And Morgan was definitely special.

Two

"Where will you berth your boat?" Morgan asked Cole as Lydia, her grandson, and the other passengers began leaving the *Anne of the Indies*.

Thinking that he, too, should be on his way, Cole was preparing a parting speech, not trusting himself to say the right thing without planning it first. In Morgan's presence he wasn't sure he could talk and think at the same time. Absently he answered her question by naming the marina where he'd arranged for a slip.

"Great," Morgan said. "That's where I keep my cruiser too." Before she could stop herself, she was offering further help instinctively, not pausing to wonder whether she wanted to spend any more time with a man whose nearness was so unsettling to her. "If you don't mind hanging around Mallory Dock until after sunset, we can go get my boat, come back for yours, and tow it to the marina. You won't find a better mechanic than the one there; he'll have your craft sea-worthy in no time."

"That's very kind of you," Cole said with careful formality, intending to turn down her offer politely.

But before he could speak, she flashed her melt-ing smile at him, and he was tongue-tied.

"It's not sentiment that makes me go to the sunset show most evenings," Morgan said, watch-ing with approval as her crew quickly and effi-ciently completed their last chores of the day. "Well, actually, I did promise Lydia's grandson Bobby I'd see him there and introduce him to the magician he saw last night, so I feel I have to show up. But usually I go out of sheer, crass commercialism. Most of the *Anne*'s passengers head straight over to Mallory Dock for the festivities, and they seem pleased when I show up. They start talking up my cruise to other people in the crowd—I see them pointing at me, especially the kids—and there's no better advertising than word-of-mouth from satisfied customers." The nervous chatter had started up again, Morgan thought, amazed at the effect Cole Jameson had on her. She laughed aloud at herself, then went on, "Besides, I have to admit I do enjoy the excitement that mounts at sun-down. It's funny. You'd think, by everyone's reac-tion, that a sunset was an extraordinary event instead of a daily, natural phenomenon."

Cole had noted that Morgan took a casual prom-ise to a child quite seriously. He was beginning to understand why so many people seemed to find her irresistible. Suddenly even he found himself opening up to Morgan. "I think what attracted me most to this town was that the people are nuts enough to celebrate sunset every night. I even like the 'crass commercialism,' to use your phrase, of the dockside T-shirt vendors and street performers."

Morgan was surprised that a man who looked so brooding, so sophisticated, would admit enjoying such corny fun. She decided she liked Cole. She was looking forward to spending part of the evening in his company.

After most of the passengers had left the ship, Morgan nodded to Cole. "We can go now."

He followed her down the gangplank like a man in a semitrance, captivated by the rippling of her soft skirt as she walked, the sparkles of sunlight reflected in her silken curls, the easy grace of her movements.

Mallory Dock was crowded with tourists and locals, the air filled with the mingled smells of burning incense, hot popcorn, and the tang of the sea. Two jugglers competed for attention with a sleight-of-hand artist, a fire-eater, a jazz guitarist, and a bongo player. Sailboats of all sizes darted back and forth on the water as if vying for a kind of center stage, directly in front of the slowly dropping, orange-red sun.

Once Morgan had located young Bobby and presented the thrilled boy to the magician he'd raved about during the day's cruise, she was free to wander around with Cole from one performer to the next, stopping long enough to enjoy a bit of each act.

Morgan noticed that Cole quietly dropped money into several hats that had been set out by the performers, and she liked him as much for trying to do it without being noticed as for his generosity. She'd established the habit of showing her appreciation to the performers just once a week, on Fridays. Since it was Wednesday, she hoped Cole didn't think she was being cheap by ignoring the hats.

Her concern over making a good impression on Cole was one of the many surprises she'd had since first encountering him. Morgan wasn't used to wondering what anyone thought of her.

"How about an orange juice?" Cole asked as they passed a brightly painted vendor's cart. "And maybe some popcorn?"

"Just a juice would be lovely," Morgan said, automatically reaching into her pocket.

Cole looked at the dollar bills she was holding out to him. "It's on me, okay? Call it a small thank-you for the rescue this afternoon."

Morgan felt a flush creep over her skin, realizing that her longstanding habit of paying her own way might have offended Cole. "Thank you," she said softly.

Cole noticed the pink tinge to her cheeks and was taken aback. Whenever he'd seen Morgan, she'd been with a coterie of males that would have aroused the envy of Scarlett O'Hara at her flirtatious best. Yet suddenly, again, she seemed shy.

A protective impulse rose up inside him. He didn't want to feel it. Those impulses only meant trouble. "Wait here," he said gruffly.

A moment later he returned with two glasses of an orange-mango concoction garnished with toothpick-speared chunks of fruit. "Come to think of it," he said, still scowling, "I think you should have dinner with me tonight. It's the least I can do to thank you."

Morgan wasn't sure why, but she bristled a little at the way he'd worded his invitation. "You don't have to take me to dinner. You've already thanked me. Several times."

"But I want to do something more," Cole said, puzzled by her answer.

"I'm only helping you the way I'm sure you'd give me a hand if my boat were in trouble," Morgan said, all at once painfully aware that she was afraid to go out to dinner with this man who threw her so badly off balance. "Anyway, I promised to meet some friends later."

"Then we'll take a rain check," Cole said, wondering even as he spoke why he wasn't accepting the easy out she was offering. He could send her flowers to show his appreciation for her help. He didn't have to get involved with her. So why did he hear himself continuing to insist? "There must be some evening in the near future when I can steal you away from all those ever-present pals of yours." He was shocked by his tone. He actually sounded resentful of her companions. Jealous.

It hit him that the expression in the enormous, amber-and-gold eyes that gazed back at him revealed sheer panic. His curiosity was aroused. Why would a woman like Morgan Sinclair act as if she were a frightened doe at the prospect of having dinner with him? "Do I look threatening or something?" he blurted out.

Morgan laughed nervously. "In a way," she murmured, then felt another flush cover her skin with crimson heat. To her relief, she heard the beginnings of a keening wail. "The bagpiper is starting up. He's great. Shall we go to the other end of the dock and listen to him?" Without waiting for an answer, Morgan started off.

Cole followed her, more intrigued than ever.

The piper was attracting a large audience, and when Morgan found a spot near enough so she could see him, there was just enough room for Cole to stand right behind her, the full length of his body almost touching hers. He chuckled, the deep sound close to her ear, sending small vibrations through her.

"It's great," he said in a tone that sent another series of pulsations through Morgan's body.

She turned her head to smile quizzically at him, wondering what had amused him, at the same time realizing with an odd thrill that she had to look up to meet his eyes. She'd never minded being as tall as most men, taller than many. Still, she was pleased that Cole's height exceeded hers by several inches. How silly, she told herself. What a ridiculous prejudice. Where was it written that a woman should be shorter than a man? Yet she couldn't deny her feelings. And they puzzled her. "What's great?" she remembered to ask.

"The piper's costume," Cole answered, grinning down at Morgan, having trouble concentrating with her lips so close to his, her body a soft invitation to his arms as they ached to fold around her. He forced himself to keep talking. "I get a kick out of the Scottish kilt and full regalia, all set off by a white muscle shirt. For some weird reason, the whole outfit looks just right in this setting.'

Morgan tore her gaze from Cole's as the expression in his dark eyes caused strange stirrings within her. "I'm sure my ancestors would approve of the shirt," she managed to say lightly. "The Scots are a practical people. Heaven knows what their natural dress would have been if the climate in Scotland had been like Key West's."

"The Scots were considered primitive savages by their enemies," Cole said, entertaining a few primitive thoughts of his own. "In a warmer climate they might have been like some of my ancestors, running around in loincloths."

Morgan tilted her head to stare at him. "You're a North American Indian, at least partly." She was stating a fact, not asking a question. Her pulse raced at the sudden vivid image that leapt into her mind of Cole dressed—or rather undressed—in the way he'd just described. He would look like a pagan god, she thought, biting down on her lower lip as her inner excitement became more difficult to control and mask.

She wasn't masking it well.

Cole watched Morgan's eyes darken to copper flames and felt her body sway toward him. Forgetting his Philadelphia manners and his determination to resist her charms, he rested his hands on her slender waist and felt the raggedness of her breathing. "I'm not sure of my Indian roots," he said, trying to keep the conversation going as a hedge against completely losing himself to the sensations Morgan was making him feel. "I can claim only a tiny drop of Seminole Indian blood in my ancestry. I do know for certain that I share a little of your Scottish heritage, Morgan. My great-grandmother was a MacLean, from Inverness."

"Well, then, you're going to love what happens at this sunset," Morgan said, allowing herself to lean back just a little, enough so her body was subtly touching Cole's. To her shock and pleasure he increased the pressure of his hands, pulled her closer, and rested his cheek against her hair.

"I already love what's happening at this sunset," he said softly.

As the sun slid behind a low-hanging cloud, sending dusty pink streaks across the sky just above the horizon, the piper began playing a slow, stately rendition of "Amazing Grace."

Cole's hands moved in opposite directions across Morgan's waist until his strong arms covered her midriff.

Her mind swirled as waves of heat poured through her, a heat unlike anything she'd ever felt before, a heat that had nothing to do with the warmth of the tropics. Instinctively she knew she could be standing in the midst of any kind of weather, and with Cole Jameson's body surrounding her as it was now, she would feel as if she were in a sheltered lagoon.

A blood red crescent sun slipped through the bottom of the cloud and touched the sea, spilling a length of metallic scarlet over the gently rippling surface. Then, slowly, the crescent became a fiery ball that extinguished itself as it sank into the ocean's depths in a last blaze of brilliant color, to the final strains of the piper's hymn.

There was a breathless silence on the dock. Morgan felt Cole's arms tighten around her, felt his heart pounding against her back.

As the crowd erupted in spontaneous applause, Morgan blinked rapidly.

Cole turned her to gaze down at her in wonder. He was astounded by the feelings that had washed over him during the past few moments. Then he saw her moist eyes. "Morgan?" he asked in a low voice.

She raised her hands to push back the threatening tears. "Pay no attention to me. I'm a sentimental dope."

"You're lovely," Cole said. "You're the loveliest woman I've ever seen in my life." Before he could stop himself, his lips captured hers in a passion-filled kiss.

"I don't understand any of this," she managed to say when he ended the kiss. "I've never—" She stopped abruptly, aware how ridiculous the truth would sound, that she'd never before experienced such an overwhelmingly beautiful moment, that she'd reached the age of twenty-eight without knowing the power of sudden, unaccountable desire, that she hadn't realized it was possible to feel so in tune with someone she hardly knew.

Cole smiled, certain he knew what Morgan had started to say. "Maybe it's Key West," he said softly, not really believing his own words, but trying to ease the almost unbearable poignance of the moment. "Or we can blame the sunset for making us overly romantic. Or the bagpipe music. Maybe tomorrow we'll laugh at ourselves."

Morgan hoped so. Or hoped not. She wasn't sure. She liked the feelings Cole aroused in her, yet she didn't know how to deal with them. She'd seen women turn to jelly over men. Their reactions had struck her as foolishly obsessive. Never had she sensed herself in danger of the same emotions. Not until she'd met Cole Jameson. "Let's go get the *Bonnie Anne*," she said, sounding more abrupt than she meant to.

Cole nodded, glad Morgan had broken the intense spell between them. The sooner they could get his boat back to the marina, the sooner he could say good night to her and go home to try to regain his sanity. "The *Bonnie Anne*," he repeated as he fell in step beside her, walking back toward Duval Street. "A reversal of Anne Bonney, Anne of the Indies, scourge of the Caribbean a couple of hundred years or so ago? Played by Jean Peters in the movie?"

Morgan flashed him her dazzling smile. "You're one of the few people I've run into who has heard of that film, or of the real woman who inspired it."

"I guess I remembered Captain Bonney because I find the idea of a lady pirate intriguing," Cole said, wishing he could stop making flirtatious remarks. He did *not* want to get involved with

Morgan Sinclair. When was he going to get that simple fact through his thick skull?

"You mentioned that your sailing school was in New Orleans," he went on, turning to a harmless topic. "Why did you launch your pirate ship in Key West?"

"The *Anne* is my second brigantine, not counting the one used in the school. I started the pirate line with the *Bonhomme Lafitte* in New Orleans." She laughed with a touch of self-deprecation. "It plies the treacherous, shark-infested waters of Lake Pontchartrain."

They reached Duval Street, and Cole spotted a cab. "I know the marina is within walking distance," he explained as he hailed the taxi. "But let's save some time."

Morgan nodded and got into the backseat of the car, wondering if Cole was as eager as he seemed to get his boat back to the marina and be rid of her. She felt she was receiving conflicting messages from him: One minute he looked at her with a gaze that brimmed with desire; the next, he seemed impersonal and uninterested.

For the first time in her life, Morgan realized, she was trying to read between the lines of what a man said, to see beneath his surface to what he was thinking, to guess at his responses to her.

Such emotional dependence was a new and uncomfortable sensation she hoped would pass, like a headache or a heat rash.

Cole gave a low whistle minutes later, when he saw Morgan's boat. "She's a beauty," he said with open admiration, determined not to succumb to the hopeless feeling that he had nothing to offer Morgan. She had everything, including a bigger and better cabin cruiser than his. But it didn't matter, he reminded himself yet again. He wasn't going to pursue her.

"She gets me where I want to go," Morgan said modestly, though she was proud of the *Bonnie Anne*. With rented equipment, a lot of elbow grease, and a mild case of the boatyard blues during the drydock period, Morgan had given her aging craft a surprisingly professional-looking paint job a few months earlier. "The *Bonnie Anne* has had a recent facelift, Cole," she said as she saw that he was mentally making a comparison between the two vessels. "Your boat's almost as big as this one. And it would look just as good with a bit of work." She stopped, frowning. "Not that I'm suggesting it needs work . . . I mean . . . it looks fine as it is, and maybe you like it . . ."

"My boat needs work," Cole said, smiling at Morgan's discomfort. He found it endearing that such an outgoing woman was so easily embarrassed. At certain moments she was like a little girl not sure how to act. "I gather from what Lydia said that you've spent a lot of time at sea," he added, unable to resist the temptation to try to learn a little more about this intriguing woman who'd robbed him of his peace of mind.

"I've been on and around boats all my life," Morgan answered as she boarded the *Bonnie Anne*. At the moment she didn't feel like telling her own life story; she was interested in Cole. "What about you?"

Cole gave a little snort of derision, unhitching the mooring ropes before hopping aboard. "I'm no sailor. I'm just a guy who dreamed of chucking everything and buying a boat. So that's what I did."

Morgan looked dubious, then spoke over her shoulder as she turned and went into the cockpit. "As I said earlier, nobody pilots a small cruiser over the rough waters you must have run into without some ability and knowledge."

"Okay, I took a course, and I practiced a little with rented boats," Cole admitted as he joined her in the cockpit. "But keep in mind that I probably broke a fuel line, so I must have done something wrong today."

"You're too hard on yourself. I can't count the busted fuel lines I've had to contend with. I don't blame myself for them, any more than I would for a flat tire on a bad road."

"You know something, Morgan Sinclair?" Cole said impulsively. "I think you're a very nice lady." He wasn't flirting this time. He was voicing a genuine belief.

Morgan smiled and lowered her gaze, utterly unequipped to deal with Cole's sweet words. She was used to rough-hewn men who showed their affection by trading insults with her.

Neither of them said much more during the short trip to Cole's boat, or on the way back to the marina. Both were lost in thought, puzzled by the power of their feelings, wary of exploring them any further.

"You're sure you won't have dinner with me?"

Cole asked when they'd returned to Duval Street in another taxi.

Morgan was tempted. So, so tempted. Being with Cole was exhilarating, a pleasure far beyond the unexciting time she'd have with her pals in some noisy bar downtown.

She frowned. Unexciting? Noisy bar? She hadn't thought about her social life in such negative terms before. Just how deeply had Cole Jameson affected her? Could she lose interest in her friends, her very existence, because of one man, as she'd seen too many women do? Could she become as obsessed over a man as those silly females did?

"Morgan, are you wavering?" Cole asked, surprised that he hoped she was.

She shook her head. "No, I really can't. I appreciate the invitation, but my friends are waiting for me."

"Another time, then?" Cole asked, resisting an impulse to drag her into his arms and kiss her again.

Morgan nodded. "Perhaps," she said softly, then hurried away before she weakened.

Cole watched her for a moment, then turned to head the opposite way, though Morgan was going in the general direction of his house. He decided he needed a long walk before going home to the empty, sprawling mansion that had been his haven of solitude until a few weeks ago, when he'd started imagining how sunlit his home would be with a golden-haired, laughing, sweet bundle of femininity gracing its impersonal rooms.

With a tightness in his loins that wouldn't go

away, and an ache in his throat that was becoming disturbingly chronic, Cole took long, loping strides through the darkened, hibiscus-bordered streets of Old Town. He gave himself a stern lecture about how important it was to guard the hassle-free existence he'd mapped out for himself when he'd chosen Key West as his new home.

Three

Effortlessly Cole maneuvered his cruiser into its berth. He gave the steering console an affectionate pat, as if to comfort his little craft for its slightly bedraggled appearance.

Cole loved his cruiser. He didn't care that it was unpretentious. It could take him to places that he'd only dreamed about until he'd succumbed to his lifelong craving for freedom and the sea. And with every passing day he was more pleased with his skill at handling the boat. Even Morgan might be impressed, he mused, then quickly tried to banish thoughts of her.

It had been five days since the night she'd towed his craft to the marina for him. Five unbelievably long days since he'd seen her—by his own choice. He'd been avoiding the places she frequented, staying away from Duval Street and Mallory Dock during the evening. It was difficult enough resisting the ghost of her that haunted him; the reality would be impossible.

As Cole cut the boat's engine his brother, who had arrived for a visit the day before, emerged from the tiny cabin, stretching his lanky body and rubbing his eyes, his dark hair disheveled, his winter-paled skin darkened by a five-o'clock shadow that nearly matched Cole's. "Hi," Doug said through a yawn. "I guess I missed most of our Sunday excursion, huh?"

"It's Monday," Cole said. "But the mistake is understandable. Time has a way of becoming meaningless down here." Rubbing a hand over his own whiskered jaw, he grinned at the thought of how annoyed his father and his uptight brother, Adam, would be to see two of the Jamesons looking like a couple of trail riders just short of payday.

The youngest Jameson hadn't managed to look truly grubby, though, Cole noted with amusement. Doug's white cotton slacks, sweatshirt, and deck shoes all bore designer insignias.

Cole loved his two younger brothers, but he didn't have much in common with either of them anymore.

"I really slept," Doug said, still bleary-eyed.

Cole hadn't been surprised or disappointed when Doug had announced he was going below for a short nap, not long after the start of their impromptu cruise.

In fact, knowing that Doug would be dead to the world for at least a couple of hours, Cole had welcomed the opportunity to zip over to his island to see how the dig was coming along—the mini-dig, he corrected himself with a small grin. Even his longtime best friend, Dan Cypress, a full-blooded Seminole Indian who was the archeologist supervising the project, held out little hope for finding anything of significance.

The excavation, based on information in an old journal that had been passed down through Cole's mother's family for a century and a half, was such a long shot in terms of potential return, it embarrassed Cole. He was almost glad secrecy was necessary to carry out the work without the nuisance of visiting curiosity seekers. It wouldn't do for anyone to know he'd sunk a tidy portion of his nest egg into such an off-the-wall project. His reputation as a canny investor might not survive the news.

"Sorry I conked out on you when you went to so much trouble to take me out on your boat," Doug said as he lowered himself to a seat just outside the cockpit, looking as sheepish as Doug was capable of looking.

"No trouble at all," Cole said cheerfully. "It's a perfectly normal reaction. The sea air will get to you every time. I warn you, now that your body has experienced true relaxation, it won't be satisfied with a cocktail lounge happy hour or even a fast run around a high rise's rooftop jogging track."

Doug grinned as he took a comb from his pocket and smoothed his straight black hair. "C'mon, Cole, you miss the action back home. Admit it."

"Spend some time with me in Key West and then say that," Cole answered, starting the task of securing the boat for the night. "You'll end up staying here, not trying to persuade me to go back to the boiler room with you."

"Boiler room? That's what you call the career you walked away from? I can't believe it. You were the best, Cole. There wasn't a stockbroker around who could match your success, including Adam and me. Dad wants you back, you know."

Cole said nothing as he battled his lingering, misplaced guilt. It wasn't as if he'd abandoned the family firm when it needed him, he reminded himself. His father was prosperous and his two brothers were doing just fine.

"Isn't a year as a dropout enough?" Doug asked after pocketing his comb.

Cole refused to let the remark go unchallenged. "I'm not a dropout," he said evenly. "I've changed my base and style of operation, that's all. My investment newsletter has a healthy subscription list, and my own portfolio is doing just fine. Now, before you open your well-meaning mouth on this subject again, hear this: I don't have a single regret for what I've left behind, and I won't be going back. Period. You can tell the folks you made your pitch but it didn't work."

To Cole's annoyance he realized he'd lost his brother's attention about halfway through his speech. Something out on the horizon had caught Doug's eye.

Cole tipped back his hat to follow Doug's gaze. Suddenly his pulse leapt. The *Anne of the Indies* was returning from its cruise.

"Beautiful," Doug murmured.

Silhouetted against the soft colors of the late-afternoon sky, the regal sailing vessel was the picture of elegance, a symbol of a bygone era when dignity counted for something.

"It looks like a pirate ship straight out of the movies," Doug said with a smile.

Cole said nothing for several minutes, simply watching the brig make for shore. At last he responded to Doug's remark. "It *is* a pirate ship straight out of the movies. It's a tourist gimmick. A day cruise with a dramatic flair. The crew members dress like pirates, or at least the old MGM costume department's idea of pirates. There are jugglers, acrobats, fencers acting out carefully choreographed battles—the works. Families line up to get on board. Kids love it."

Doug laughed. "Kids of what age? I think it would be a real hoot to go on a cruise like that. I mean, the sea itself is okay, but it gets kind of boring. When you've seen one wave, you've seen them all, right?"

"Right," Cole drawled. Doug had been with him only a few hours, and already Cole realized there was no point trying to convey to him the lure of the ocean, the joy of a life of peace and quiet.

Doug accepted Cole's agreement and already becoming bored, began kicking the ball of his foot against the deck, a gesture of impatience he'd had since childhood.

But Cole was only dimly aware of his brother's restlessness. He picked up his spyglasses and scanned the *Anne*'s deck until he found what he was looking for, half-convinced that his imagination had exaggerated the improbable apricot of Morgan's curls, the luster of skin that looked as if someone had dipped a brush into the sun and burnished her with its gold, the appeal of lips that were a clear, soft pink even without cosmetic help.

"What are you looking at?" Doug asked.

Cole still didn't answer. A playful breeze had lifted the hem of Morgan's filmy red skirt, offering Cole a glimpse of bare, tanned legs so long and shapely, they took his breath away.

The burning heat that coiled within him made it painfully clear that avoiding Morgan had intensified his desire for her.

"What the hell is so interesting?" Doug demanded.

Abruptly Cole lowered the binoculars. "Nothing," he answered. "Let's finish up here, and then I'll give you the fifty-cent tour of my town."

"*Your* town? You're pretty possessive all of a sudden," Doug remarked with a quizzical smile.

Cole thought of Morgan. Possessiveness was what she aroused in him. It made no sense at all. He wasn't a possessive man—never had been at any rate. But he wanted Morgan all to himself.

"Hey, this *is* my town," Cole said with forced cheer. "I'm not here by accident. I chose the place as my new home. After you've had a good look at Margaritaville, you just might feel the same way."

Cole headed straight for Mallory Dock, knowing Morgan would be there. With any luck Doug wouldn't spot her in the crowd. Even if he did, and even if he made a play for her, maybe she wouldn't be like most females who fell for his lines. Whatever was going to happen, Cole decided, it might as well happen right away, while he was with Doug and could keep an eye on him. Besides, he thought, a visit to Key West without taking in the sunset celebrations would be unthinkable.

Aware that he was rationalizing, knowing he couldn't stay away from Morgan any longer, Cole led his brother toward the waterfront, his eyes constantly peeled for that special tumble of golden curls glinting in the setting sun.

"What's the rush?" Doug asked.

Cole realized he'd quickened his pace considerably. "There's a lot to see," he answered. "And sunset's on the way."

"Sunset? So what?"

Cole shook his head. "So what? Kid, that's a typical fast-track attitude we're going to change tonight."

"Not likely," Doug said, though he kept up with Cole without grumbling.

They reached Mallory Dock before sunset, when the performers and the crowds were at their peak.

Doug grinned. "This is great. I feel like a kid again."

"You've never stopped being a kid," Cole teased. An instant later his pulse quickened. Out of nowhere Morgan had appeared, walking toward him, though she didn't see him. She was talking and laughing with the petite, redheaded juggler from her pirate crew.

Cole's heart pounded violently and the blood raced through his veins with unbelievable heat. But he kept walking, pretending to be casual.

"Hey, now there's something I could really go for!" Doug suddenly said, looking right at Morgan and the other girl.

Every muscle in Cole's body tightened and his hands instinctively clenched. The familiar, inexplicable shaft of possessiveness gripped him. "What could you really go for?" he asked tightly.

"That redhead over there. The one with the tall blonde," Doug answered. "The Amazon's gorgeous, but I prefer petite women."

Though Cole relaxed considerably, he was shocked by the barrage of emotions battering him. His feelings toward Morgan had been straining at their tight reins since the first time he'd seen her. All at once they were like a team of runaway horses, and he couldn't seem to regain control of them.

He searched desperately for some flaw in the woman that would turn him off, or at least temper his response to her, but he found nothing. Even Doug's suggestion that she was larger than life didn't help. Cole liked the aura of strength Morgan emanated. It fired his blood, filling his mind with vivid, earthy visions of how it would feel to have her in his arms, her voluptuous body crushed under his, her long legs wrapped tightly around him.

She looked up and saw him. Their gazes met and held for a moment that was a suspension of time and place. His heartbeat thundering by now, louder and more syncopated than the wild thrumming of the bongo player in the background, Cole tried to smile, sure everyone on the dock could hear what was going on inside him.

Morgan felt as if someone had just crashed into her, knocking the breath out of her body, making her heart stop and then start racing as if to catch up on the missed beats.

She tried to tear her gaze from the dark eyes that were caressing her skin with a warmth that turned her insides to molten liquid.

Other men had looked at her with unmistakable desire. No one but Cole Jameson had turned that desire into a compelling magnetism that destroyed all her defenses.

"Hi," she said in a small voice, her breathing labored, her hands clenched by her sides so Cole couldn't see her trembling. The violence of her body's response to the man was almost frightening.

"Hi," he answered softly, searching for something more to say. Anything. Just so she wouldn't see the profound effect she had on him. "How's the cruise going?"

"It's sold out every day," Morgan answered, wondering how Cole could be so casual when his impact on her was so dramatic. Didn't he feel any of what she was experiencing?

"What cruise?" Doug asked, flashing one of his best grins, clearly pleased by the unexpected bonus of getting a chance to meet the little redhead.

"That pirate ship you saw earlier," Cole explained without looking at Doug, keeping his gaze fixed on Morgan as though afraid she might disappear if he glanced away. "This lady is its captain." He blinked, remembering his manners long enough to spare a quick glance for the smaller woman. "And her friend is a talented member of its crew." With his gaze on Morgan again, he introduced Doug.

Morgan followed Cole's lead and introduced her companion.

"So now I know what you were peering at for so long through your binoculars," Doug said. "Shame, big brother, for not sharing."

Cole thought about strangling him, but Doug quickly moved away, somehow managing to draw the redhead along with him.

"Your brother looks like you," Morgan said, though she wasn't sure how she knew. She'd hardly glimpsed the younger man.

"People often comment on the resemblance," Cole answered. "I have another brother. Adam. He doesn't look like either of us. He has my father's lighter coloring. Doug and I are throwbacks to some obscure ancestry on my mother's side." Stupid, he told himself fiercely. How stupid he was to ramble on this way, and even worse to refer to those roots of his again. Why did he blurt out whatever popped into his mind when he was around Morgan? Why hadn't he picked up a little of Doug's smoothness? Shouldn't the oldest brother in a family be the one with the savoir faire?

Morgan managed a tiny smile. "Then the Seminole blood comes from your mother's side."

"Or the Spanish blood. Or both. As I said, we aren't sure. You seem awfully fascinated with the possibility of my Indian heritage, Morgan."

"Because it's awfully fascinating," she answered, liking the sound of her name on his lips—his perfectly sculpted, tempting lips. "Even more so because you aren't sure. I sense a real story. I love stories."

"How about this one, then?" he said with a rush of fierce need to tell her what he felt. "How about a story of a man who can't stop thinking about a beautiful pirate, even though he doesn't want to think about her?"

"Why doesn't he want to?" Morgan asked, her eyes widening as his blunt statement caught her off guard.

"Because . . ." Cole lifted his hat and raked his fingers through his hair, laughing quietly. "'I don't know why. When he's with her he can't remember.'"

"Then the reason mustn't be very important," Morgan murmured as they started walking. She wondered why she was encouraging him, even coaxing him to pursue what was happening between them. Clearly, he didn't want it to happen. Neither did she. Did she?

As if tugged along by an unseen hand, Cole found himself following Morgan until he was standing directly behind her in the crowd surrounding a talented busker, just as he'd stood behind her the week before to listen to the Scottish piper. Once again he was close enough to breathe in her delicate fragrance as they listened together to the cool, sweet harmonies.

"You like jazz?" he asked when the musician paused between numbers.

Morgan turned her head to answer him. "I'm

not the connoisseur my sister Lisa is, but I—"
She stopped, all at once overcome, as if she'd
been deprived of oxygen. Swallowing hard, she
blinked several times, trying to recover from the
shock of finding him so close to her again. It was
nerve-wracking. He was like a sleek, silent cat.
Black and mysterious and lethal.

"Hi, again," Cole said with a tentative smile.

"Hi," Morgan answered after several seconds.
Then she blurted out in a husky whisper, "What's
happening between us? Or is my imagination running wild?" Even as she spoke she had to resist
an urge to reach up and touch Cole's scratchy
cheek.

"You're not imagining anything, Morgan. And I
wish I could explain what's happening. The simple truth of the matter is that you've been driving
me crazy since you came to Key West."

Morgan's whole body went weak as the oddly
raspy sound of his deep voice sent delicious shiv-
ers through her. "Me too!" she said, then realized
her comment didn't sound right. "I mean, you
too? I mean . . . what I'm trying to say is—"

A huge, tattooed hand descended on her head
and ruffled her hair.

"Hi, Cueball," Morgan said, managing a feeble
grin for her buddy, though she wished he had
chosen a more opportune moment to appear on
the scene.

With a baleful glare at the intruder he recog-
nized as a biker who was one of Morgan's more
offbeat friends, Cole nodded to the man, deciding
that Cueball was well named. Totally bald, he

looked as if he'd been born and raised in a pool hall.

Not overly tall, the biker was nevertheless impressive. His body bore a distinct resemblance to a half-ton truck, his face to something the truck had run over.

Since the first time he'd seen Cueball with Morgan, Cole had been at a loss to figure out the exact relationship between the two. The one thing he was beginning to understand with perfect clarity was that getting a chance to be alone with Morgan for any length of time was going to be a major challenge.

He wished he'd taken better advantage of the privacy they'd had on the *Bonnie Anne*. There were so many questions he could have asked her, so many ways he could have gotten to know her a little better.

Morgan wondered if introductions were in order. She decided they probably were. "Cole, this is my friend Cueball. Cueball, meet Cole Jameson."

Cueball's great hand closed over Cole's, but squeezed with surprising gentleness. "Hey, man. I think I seen you around a few times. You're the guy that keeps to himself and makes everybody around town wonder what you're up to."

Taken aback by the comment, and by Cueball's smile—his teeth looked as if they'd pried off their share of bottle caps—Cole just stared at the man.

"You were away for a while, right?" Cueball asked.

"Yes, for a couple of weeks," Cole answered. It hadn't occurred to him that the locals would notice his activities. It was something to think about. Even to worry about.

Cueball's interest was already straying. "It looks like the fire-eater's got a good crowd tonight. I think I'll go see if I can shake him up."

Morgan laughed softly. "If anyone can, Cueball, it's you."

Cueball nodded and started working his way through the crowd, glancing back at Morgan just before he was out of earshot. "I'll see you later at Captain Tony's."

"Right," Morgan yelled, then smiled nervously at Cole.

It was odd, she thought. Shyness had never been a problem for her. Her parents had taught their daughters that most strangers were potential friends, and Morgan had taken the lesson to heart. Usually she was completely at ease with anyone in any situation.

Yet with Cole Jameson, she personified awkwardness. Her brain stalled, and her tongue was barely capable of forming syllables.

Aware of Morgan's momentary distress, he smiled at her. "We were saying?"

Morgan's sense of humor came to the rescue. "Not much of anything, at least in my case. I usually don't trip over my tongue that way."

"I usually don't greet a woman I hardly know by telling her she's been driving me crazy. Of course, I've never had cause before." Cole had abandoned his plan to battle his attraction to Morgan. It was a fight that had been lost before it had begun. "Do you think we should get together to talk about this whole situation?" He grinned. "Maybe over that dinner I still owe you?"

In the brief hesitation before Morgan opened her mouth to reply, the guitarist started into another number with a great flourish. At the same time, Doug appeared at Cole's elbow, and two little girls ran up to Morgan, possessively dragging her away amid squeals that the Captain *had* to see the performing dog on the other side of the square.

Once again feeling infuriatingly helpless, Cole watched Morgan disappear into the crowd, realizing just how much competition for her attention he was up against.

He comforted himself with the fact that he knew she was going to Captain Tony's bar later—to meet Cueball, unfortunately.

Doug was ready to move on. "How about going for a drink? At Jimmy Buffett's Margaritaville Cafe, for instance."

"The redhead's going to be there, right?"

"How did you know, big brother?"

Cole rolled his eyes. "I *am* your big brother, that's how. But we're not leaving here yet. The sun still hasn't set. Let's wait for it, okay?"

Doug gave him a sly grin. "And you haven't made it to first base with the Amazon. Sure, Cole. I'll stick around to give you another chance with her. I can't say I blame you. She sure is a tall one, though. I'd never have guessed you'd go for that type. Angie was so little and fragile—" Abruptly Doug stopped. "Sorry. I know you don't like me to talk about her."

"That's right," Cole said forcefully. "I don't."

Doug shifted uncomfortably from one foot to

the other. "I feel I have to tell you something. Angie's remarried."

"Good for her." Cole's expression betrayed no emotion.

"There's more," Doug said, pausing to clear his throat. "She's . . . she's pregnant."

A muscle in Cole's jaw tightened, but he said nothing.

"She took you for such a ride," Doug burst out in a low voice that vibrated with long-suppressed anger. "And you let her do it. She left you. She'd been blatantly unfaithful, yet you gave her the house, a big settlement, a quick and easy divorce—"

"It's behind me. Ancient history," Cole pointed out.

"Not so ancient," Doug argued. "Angie's the reason you're having a midlife crisis."

Suddenly Cole turned to gape at his brother, almost laughing out loud, amazed that Doug understood so little about him. "Once and for all, I am *not* having a midlife crisis. And Angie and I split two years ago. Don't you realize what a favor she did me? Our marriage hadn't worked from the beginning. No matter how hard we both tried, it was a lost cause. I gave her the house and a settlement because she had no career. I could rebuild. She couldn't. You can say she took me for a ride if you like, but I consider the divorce arrangements perfectly fair. And if she's happy now, she has my blessing."

Doug wasn't satisfied. "Look, Cole, anyone who knows you has your number. Your heart's too big for your own good. You're a giver, not a taker."

With a brief twinkle in his eyes Doug added, "Okay, who am I to talk when I've taken advantage of you all my life, right? But dammit, how can you be so calm about Angie? Didn't she insist she didn't want children, even when she knew how much you looked forward to starting a family? Now she's basking in the attention, playing little mother as if she were born to the role."

Cole couldn't deny that the news of his ex-wife's changed attitude about motherhood hurt, but he reminded himself that it was mainly his pride that had taken a beating when she'd left him for another man, and it was his pride that stung now. "Angie was right not to want kids with me. Our marriage wasn't strong enough," he said quietly, then clamped his hand down on Doug's shoulder and smiled. He appreciated his brother's loyalty, if not the painful reminders of his own sorry failure to provide his former wife with the security and happiness another man had managed to give her. "What do you want me to do, kid? Go back to Philadelphia and demand a refund on the settlement because Angie's found contentment?"

"No," Doug said gruffly. "I just want you to come back, that's all. And I think she's the reason you won't."

Cole slowly shook his head. "She isn't. I'm not going back because I'm where I belong. It's as simple as that, Doug. Accept it. Let go of your resentment of Angie. I did, a long time ago. Now, please, Doug, can we just have a good time together this week?" He waved his hand toward a gaggle of pretty young women a few feet away. "As they say, kid, so many women, so little time. Don't waste any of it on useless arguments."

Doug grinned, giving in at last.

But Cole suddenly felt drained. Though he hadn't lied to Doug about his feelings—or rather, his lack of feelings—for his former wife, dredging up the past had brought back all the reasons he'd vowed to avoid romantic involvement.

Doug had said he was a giver. Cole wasn't sure. He hadn't been able to give Angela what she'd needed, and he still wasn't sure how or why he'd fallen short.

What, then, could he hope to offer a woman like Morgan Sinclair?

He decided that he and Doug wouldn't make it to Captain Tony's this particular evening. He'd be doing Morgan a favor if he just stayed away from her.

Four

A week and a half had passed since the *Anne of the Indies* had gone to Cole Jameson's rescue, and apart from their meeting at Mallory Dock on Monday evening, Morgan hadn't seen Cole in all that time.

She couldn't help wondering if he was a bit of a game player, a Don Juan type who couldn't resist trying to get a woman interested in him even if he didn't want to pursue the attraction, just to feed his own ego.

Cole hadn't struck her as that shallow or selfish, but the things he'd said to her certainly didn't jibe with his actions.

Impatient with her inability to shake Cole from her thoughts, Morgan decided to go for a quiet, solitary Sunday cruise on the *Bonnie Anne*. The brilliantly sunny day was too beautiful to be spent indoors, and going alone to a beach crowded with couples and contented families wasn't her idea of relaxation.

But she didn't have a relaxing day. She had a miserable one. And it made her angry that she'd given Cole Jameson the power to affect her so deeply.

Hours later, in her rented cottage several blocks from the heart of Old Town, she sat curled up in an overstuffed chintz-and-rattan chair, fiercely battling a melancholy mood that was so foreign to her, she wasn't sure how to handle it.

She was being a child, she told herself. No. Worse than a child. Children were too busy enjoying life to be dumb enough to mess it up with . . . whatever she was messing hers up with. It certainly couldn't be love. She didn't know Cole Jameson, so she didn't love him. Simple. So what was her problem? Why the misery because one man, a man she barely knew, was toying with her emotions? She had lots and lots of wonderful friends. Why should she care about him? Why the self-pity that kept rolling over her in waves? It wasn't like her to feel self-pity. It wasn't like her to feel any of the seesawing, obsessive emotions she'd been experiencing over Cole Jameson.

Therefore, she concluded, Cole Jameson was bad news.

Suddenly she decided that a chat with one of her sisters would be a balm to her frayed nerves.

She picked up the receiver and started to punch out Stefanie's number in New Orleans, then abruptly stopped.

Stefanie wouldn't do her frame of mind much good, she remembered. And Steffie didn't need to be troubled by a less-than-cheery call from Key West. Steffie herself had run aground on the treacherous shoals of love just months earlier. Lord, the woman had gone so far as to get married! To elope, for heaven's sake!

And Steffie hadn't been herself since the marriage had fallen apart within weeks of the wedding day.

Perhaps talking to Lisa would be fun, Morgan thought, but pulled back before she'd gotten past the first numbers that would connect her with southern France. She remembered that Lisa was getting over a relationship with a saxophone player who'd given her the runaround.

What was wrong with the Sinclair women? After years of blissful independence, suddenly they were falling prey to the wrong men.

Well, there was one holdout, as far as Morgan knew. Heather hadn't stumbled yet. But she was only twenty-two and still believed in fairy-tale love and happy endings—along with ghosts and second sight and little people.

Morgan only hoped that some handsome Scot wouldn't ride into Edinburgh and carry her baby sister off to his castle to break her trusting heart. At this point, Heather was the only Sinclair daughter whose heart was still intact.

Slowly replacing the receiver, Morgan confronted herself with the realization that she didn't consider her own heart intact.

Cole Jameson had invaded it. And he'd made it clear he didn't want to be there.

Morgan decided she was going to shake off her lovesickness the way she would beat a nasty flu. She couldn't cure it by taking two aspirin and drinking lots of fluids, but she had her own medicine: Work.

The initial data had come in from the market research consultant she'd hired. Now was as good a time as any to study the feasibility reports about adding a third ship, this one in the Bahamas, to her tiny but fast-growing line. If all went well, within a couple of months the Key West cruise could get along without her, and she could move on to the next adventure.

There would be no Cole Jameson in Nassau, which suited Morgan perfectly.

With a determined set to his jaw, Cole headed for the pier where the *Anne of the Indies* had just docked. He'd been doing a lot of thinking, and he'd made his decision: Morgan Sinclair was worth going after, whatever came of it. As far as disappointing her was concerned, what had he been doing so far?

Morgan strode down the brigantine's gangplank, a bit tired but pleased with the way the day had gone.

As she reached the dock, she spied her daylong, youthful adversary waiting for her. "En garde, Captain Morgan," shouted the excited nine-year-old named Jamie, who had dogged her heels throughout the cruise, never seeming to tire of the game of mock swordplay.

For perhaps the tenth time Morgan threw back her head and mimed a furious exchange of thrusts and parries with the youngster. Then, tired and looking forward to a long soak in a hot tub, she clutched her heart and played a brief dying scene that earned a smattering of applause from the tourists watching the playful skirmish.

"Aw, gee," Jamie said, realizing that his afternoon of fun was about to come to an end.

"You're too good for me," Morgan told him. "I didn't have a chance."

"I could teach you," the boy suggested eagerly.

His father came to the rescue. "Let the poor captain rest in peace, James. It was a wonderful day, but it's time to pack it in, okay?"

"Aw, gee," Jamie repeated. But with a wistful smile at Morgan, he trailed obediently after his parents.

"See ya," Morgan called after him, then turned to head home, taking off her large hoop earrings and pocketing them.

What a ham she was, Cole thought. What a beautiful, lovable ham.

He watched Morgan's every move as she strode along the pier toward him. He liked the way her electric-blue skirt and the lace petticoat under it swirled around her long legs as she walked, the way her bright yellow blouse, with its billowing sleeves and loose cut, failed to hide her luxurious curves. A bold pink sash at her narrow waist matched her flat sandals; she looked like a tropical garden in full bloom.

Only a certain kind of woman could carry off

such bold styles and brilliant splashes of color, Cole reflected, and Morgan Sinclair was definitely that kind: Tall, confident, innately sensual. Her hips swayed in an easy rhythm, as though she moved to music only she could hear.

Morgan was looking out to sea as she walked and didn't notice Cole until she almost ran into him.

"Hi," he said, falling into step beside her.

She hesitated only a fraction of a second, then made herself smile. Cole was clean-shaven, dressed in white linen slacks and a crisp blue shirt, and was minus his shabby hat. He looked as appealing as ever, in a totally different way. "Hi," she said, managing to sound casual. But then she couldn't think of anything else to say. She walked a little faster.

Cole easily kept up, though he noticed the accelerated pace. He took a deep breath and plunged right in. "I'm sorry I've been such a jerk. I've meant every word I've said about . . . about the way I feel about you. You must be wondering why I haven't *done* anything."

Morgan was tempted to pretend she hadn't noticed, but being coy wasn't in her. Besides, Cole's honesty deserved as much in return. "I've been puzzled," she admitted. "But I thought perhaps I'd read too much into one kiss and a few meaningful glances, and perhaps into some of what you'd said to me. I'm not very experienced at this sort of thing."

"What sort of thing?" Cole asked.

She laughed. "I'm so inexperienced, I'm not sure.

I think we've been conducting an on-again, off-again flirtation, but I could be mistaken."

"You're not mistaken," he said quietly. "I haven't been doing a very good job of it, though."

"On the contrary, Cole. You've been doing a *very* good job of it, if the object of the exercise was to arouse my interest and then totally confuse me."

"I'm kind of confused myself." He frowned, realizing they were virtually racing along the street. "Are you in a big hurry?"

She stopped in her tracks and glared at him. "Are you suggesting I'm trying to nudge you into some kind of . . . of relationship?"

It took Cole a moment to understand. Then, splaying his fingers and pushing them through his hair, he sighed heavily. "I only meant that you're walking awfully fast, Morgan."

She closed her eyes and tilted back her head to feel the sun on her face, hoping it would calm her down so she wouldn't make a fool of herself again.

Cole was tempted to reach for her, to span her waist with his hands and draw her closer, close enough so he could kiss her eyelids and brush his mouth over her cheeks and lips and throat.

But he didn't move, he simply gazed at her, imagining the silkiness and warmth of her.

Finally Morgan opened her eyes and faced Cole. "As I said, I haven't had much experience. Sorry."

"Well, *are* you in a hurry? Walking, I mean?" Cole asked softly, a dull ache throbbing inside him as Morgan's delicate fragrance tantalized his senses and her golden-brown eyes drew him into their depths.

Morgan shook her head. She couldn't speak. Cole's expression had become so sensual, so tender, she felt as if he were making love to her right where they stood. It was an amazing moment. She almost felt the steely strength of his arms around her, the hardness of his chest, the ripple of taut muscle under his skin. His lips seemed to possess hers, his gaze stripping away all barriers, his hands waiting patiently for her breasts to fill them. Morgan felt her breathing become ragged, in cadence with the rise and fall of his chest, the rhythm of the ocean in the distance.

She felt she had to do something to break the spell. "Why are you confused?" she asked Cole, remembering his earlier remark.

"Because of mistakes I've made, mistakes I don't want to make again. Where are you going right now? Aren't you planning to take in the sunset?"

Morgan looked down. "I'm afraid I've been skipping it lately. I'm letting my crew members do that particular bit of public relations."

Cole remembered the sunset they'd shared, the lush feel of her in his arms. His body responded to the memory with a rush of need that was difficult to ignore. Cupping his hand under her elbow, he gently guided her to start walking again.

"Where are you headed now?" he asked Morgan as they turned onto a quiet side street. Selfishly he was hoping he could keep her to himself for a while.

"I . . . I was planning to go home. I'd like to change my clothes and grab a quick bite to eat before I go to meet the gang."

"Do you meet your buddies every single night, Morgan?"

She smiled, suspecting what Cole was leading up to. "Not every night. But fairly often. It's an unusual habit for me to have developed, because I've never made a practice of hanging around bars. For some reason, the ones here in Key West seem more like community centers."

"Could I talk you into going for that dinner of ours tonight, instead?"

Morgan bit down on her lower lip, wishing she hadn't made a promise to Cueball. "I'm afraid I have to show up for a little while. At that new place on Duval, the one near Eaton Street that just opened last week."

Cole realized he'd lost touch with the dating scene. He wasn't sure whether he was getting the brush-off or whether Morgan really was regretful. "How about later?" he asked, taking a chance. "We could go to the bar, then head for . . ." His words trailed off. He didn't want to seem presumptuous. "I mean, unless you . . ."

"I'd love it," Morgan answered.

Cole stopped walking, took his hand from his pocket, and lightly touched Morgan's arm so that she stopped too. "What did you say?" he asked.

"I'd love to have dinner with you," Morgan said, her voice soft, her smile the sweetest Cole had ever seen.

He felt his body responding to the shining amber of Morgan's eyes, the rich curve of her lips. "Why change clothes?" he asked, reluctant to let her go. "You look terrific."

Morgan glowed at Cole's words. She found herself wanting to look as terrific as she possibly could, just to please him. "Thank you," she said, already wondering what she would wear. "I appreciate the compliment, but after a strenuous day on the ship, it's nice to get out of these things, have a fast shower . . ." The darkening of Cole's eyes told Morgan she'd wandered into dangerous territory. "And put on a fresh dress," she added in a breathless voice, her own desire kindled by the sudden flare of passion in Cole's gaze.

"You always wear dresses," Cole said, still standing in the middle of the sidewalk, staring at Morgan. "I've never seen you in jeans or shorts."

"I do wear jeans. Just not in public in Key West," Morgan answered, absently thinking they were having a rather odd conversation. She'd never pictured Cole as a man who noticed or cared about a woman's clothes. "When I decided to play the role of pirate queen, I went for a feminine look instead of trying to imitate a man."

"It was a wise decision," Cole said, his lips quirking in a smile. "You'd never make it as a man."

Morgan felt the familiar flush creep over her throat and cheeks. "Anyway," she went on, "since Key West is a small town, I thought I should keep up the image all the time."

"Captain Morgan, Pirate Queen," Cole said with a grin. "You play the role perfectly, even to the *Captain Blood* music on your stereo system."

Morgan laughed. "I refuse to apologize for the taped music. I always thought life should come equipped with background music. Maybe Hollywood has spoiled us, but it seems to me that half the disappointments in life—the kiss that isn't anything like the ones on the silver screen, for instance—are a letdown because the violins are missing."

Unconcerned about passersby, Cole gave in to an irresistible impulse. With slow, deliberate movements he curled his fingers around Morgan's shoulders and drew her close, bending his head until he could brush his mouth over hers, unable to resist stroking her full lower lip with the tip of his tongue before he forced himself to pull away. He was intoxicated by the tantalizing taste of her, encouraged by the way her eyes remained closed, her head tilted back as if she were waiting for another kiss, her hands moving up to lie flat against his chest. "I don't know, Morgan," he murmured. "I could swear I just heard a whole string section in the background."

"An entire philharmonic," Morgan answered with a deep sigh, her eyes still closed because she was afraid if she opened them, the symphony of pleasure would stop.

Cole couldn't resist her invitation. He lowered his head once more, summoning iron control as he touched his lips to Morgan's again, this time not daring to explore even slightly with his tongue. "What time should I meet you?" he asked as he forced himself to draw away.

Morgan gave another long, shaky sigh, amazed that a simple kiss could make her want so much more. Reluctantly she opened her eyes. "I'd say . . ." It was difficult for her to focus, let alone think clearly. Finally she calculated the time she would need. "It'll take me about an hour." Remembering that she had private business with Cueball, she added some leeway. "Maybe an hour and a half."

"Then I'll join you in ninety minutes," Cole said, dropping a kiss to the tip of her nose before releasing her.

Morgan watched him walk quickly away. Then she turned and hurried toward her cottage, still haunted by the music Cole had made her hear.

Cole hesitated at the doorway of the glitzy new bar while his eyes adjusted to the darkened interior.

Sitting at a large round table with Juan Fernandez, the weathered old cigarmaker who was her best friend in Key West and a sort of self-appointed surrogate father, Morgan saw Cole and felt as if an outside force had illuminated the dim room.

With a blue linen jacket added to the white slacks and paler blue shirt he'd been wearing earlier, Cole was devastatingly attractive.

Yet it struck Morgan that the man was still a mystery to her. She knew almost nothing about him, except that when he was near, she felt more alive than when he wasn't.

As Cole's glance swept the room and came to rest on Morgan, she discovered, to her surprise, that she was nervous, a sensation only he seemed capable of arousing in her.

Trying to laugh at her disturbing response to

Cole's purposeful advance, Morgan silently kidded herself that she should have worn something in leopard skin to reflect her mood, not the pink confection she'd chosen, with its off-the-shoulder, deeply ruffled neckline and full skirt.

But her humor faded as Cole's gaze moved over her and she suddenly became aware of the fine, soft cotton of her dress caressing her skin, the tips of her breasts hardening and thrusting against the thin material.

Cole reached the table and stood absolutely still for a moment, smiling down at Morgan. He could barely resist the urge to sweep her up in his arms and carry her off to his private garden, where he could have her to himself amid the heady scent of frangipani and sea air stirred by the mingling waters of the Atlantic Ocean and the Gulf of Mexico.

He realized he was being a bit premature. A whole evening alone with Morgan was ahead. For the moment he had to keep a firm grip on his libido—no matter what Morgan's smooth, enticing shoulders did to his imagination.

Unfortunately, things didn't turn out quite the way he'd hoped.

First, Morgan couldn't leave the bar right away. She said she had to wait to talk with Cueball, who hadn't shown up yet.

With a great deal of willpower Cole refrained from asking why his dinner date with Morgan had to be delayed because of a prior commitment to a tardy biker.

Then Juan decided to quiz Cole as if he were a Victorian father interviewing his daughter's suitor in the library. "You have been living in Key West for close to a year," the cigarmaker said, not mincing words. "Perhaps it would surprise you to learn that you have aroused the curiosity of your neighbors here."

It struck Cole that Juan might be interested in more than Morgan's romantic involvement. "Cueball mentioned the same thing," Cole said, hoping he sounded indifferent to local gossip. "I had no idea my activities would interest anyone."

Sensing the strange undercurrent between Juan and Cole, Morgan hastened to smooth things over. "Juan tells me privacy is the one thing Conchs can't tolerate," she said with a soft laugh. "They don't much care what goes on in their little town, as long as they know about it."

"I'm disappointed," Cole said smoothly. "For a moment I was flattered that Conchs were interested in an outsider like me. Now you say it's just a matter of general policy. What's everyone drinking, by the way?" he asked, getting up to go to the bar for a round. He glanced at the empty bottles on the table. "Another Dos Equis, Juan? And a cola for you, Morgan?"

She smiled, taken aback. "How did you know?"

"I've noticed that you always alternate between alcoholic and nonalcoholic drinks," Cole answered, not even attempting to hide how closely he'd watched her over the past weeks.

He felt Juan's gaze boring into his back as he stood at the bar waiting for service. Though he appreciated the man's protectiveness toward Morgan, he wasn't too pleased to be the object of local conjecture.

Returning to the table with beer for Juan and himself, and a cola with a wedge of lime in it for Morgan, Cole noticed that Cueball had arrived at last.

The biker made a beeline for Morgan. Cole pretended not to notice when, after a bit of small talk, Morgan casually handed Cueball an envelope, shushing him when he tried to offer his thanks.

Clearly the woman was a soft touch, Cole mused.

His conclusion was confirmed moments later—and the final blow dealt to the evening's plans—when a young girl wandered into the bar and looked around until she spied Morgan. She approached the table, chewing on her lower lip and twisting a lock of her long, mousy-blond hair around one finger. "Captain Morgan?" she asked in a voice barely above a whisper.

Morgan looked up at the newcomer, sensing trouble. Not tonight, she begged silently. Please, not tonight!

"My name's Mary-Ann?" the girl said, her rising inflection making a question out of the statement. "I'm sort of in trouble, and somebody said maybe you'd help me?"

Morgan's heart sank. For just an instant she wished people would refer needy souls elsewhere. But when Mary-Ann's eyes filled with tears, Morgan smiled. "Hey, c'mon. Whatever the problem is, we can solve it. Here, sit down, and let's talk."

Morgan half-expected Cole to get up and walk out of the bar and wouldn't have blamed him if he had. But he surprised her by making a quick change in their plans, buying tacos, chili dogs, and burgers at the bar's food counter, and being sympathetic but firm, giving clearheaded advice to the girl. Mary-Ann, who was nineteen but didn't have the street smarts of some five-year-olds, had run away from home with her boyfriend because her strict parents had forbidden her to see him. The young man had dumped her after they'd had a tiff, leaving her without money, friends, or a place to stay.

Morgan was amazed at how quickly Cole persuaded the waif to phone her parents and reassure them she was all right. And when it became clear that Mary-Ann's best option was to stay with Morgan overnight then catch a morning bus out of town, Cole cheerfully walked them home.

By the time the girl had gone inside, leaving her benefactors to say good night on the front porch, Morgan knew Cole was a special sort of man, the kind it would be difficult not to love.

Yet despite his acceptance of their ruined plans, Morgan sensed Cole's withdrawal from her. "I'm sorry about the way things turned out," she said.

"Things turned out the way they should have," Cole answered, taking one of her hands and raising it to brush his lips over her fingers. "You know, I had every intention of trying to seduce you tonight, and I think I might have succeeded. But then I saw what a giving, trusting, beautiful person you are, and I realized you deserve better than an affair with a burnt-out stockbroker who hasn't a whole lot to offer you. I can't resist you, Morgan. I ache for you. I can't stay away from you for very long or get you out of my mind when I'm not with you . . ." He shook his head, embarrassed by his garbled speech. "I guess what I'm doing is warning you that getting entangled with me might not be such a good idea."

Morgan had trouble understanding what he was trying to accomplish. Some of his words thrilled her, others made her insides twist into a knot of apprehension. Did he want her or not? She couldn't tell for certain. She was too straightforward herself to cope well with confusion and complexity. "A stockbroker?" she murmured irrelevantly, not sure what else to say at this point. "It's the last thing I'd have guessed that you'd do for a living."

Her comment brought home to Cole just how little she knew about him. For that matter, he hadn't learned much about her. He smiled. Why was he trying to make long-term decisions about what they could mean to each other? In fact, why was he taking on all the decisions himself in the first place? Why couldn't he let Morgan decide whether she wanted to get involved with him? Why not take the time to get to know Morgan properly and see how things developed? Obviously, part of him was still racing along the kind of fast track he'd been used to in Philadelphia. "Let's start by becoming friends," he suggested gently.

Friends, Morgan repeated silently. Friends. What she felt for him went far, far beyond simple friendship. But she nodded. "Good idea," she said with an effort at a smile. Her pride made her add, "You needn't have worried too much about trying to seduce me, though. It wouldn't have happened, no matter how many violins I heard when you kissed me. I've never been seduced, and I hope I never will be." She leaned forward, gave him a peck on the cheek, removed her hands from his, and stepped inside her house. "See ya," she said lightly, then closed the door.

Cole stood rooted to the spot for several moments, stunned by her quick exit, trying to figure out what she'd meant. She'd never been seduced? Surely she'd been involved somewhere along the way.

He decided there was nothing to be gained by standing on her porch puzzling over her words. Walking slowly back to the mansion that seemed more cavernous and empty than ever, Cole told himself he'd done the right thing by not trying to rush Morgan into an affair.

The problem was, he didn't *feel* right about it. He just felt lonely.

Five

For the next few nights Cole saw little of Morgan, though he spent a fair amount of time downtown.

He knew he could be more aggressive in his pursuit. He could call her. He could meet her when the *Anne* docked. He could go knocking on the door of her cottage.

But he felt he should approach her more casually, get to know her in her own setting, among her friends.

The trouble was, Morgan wasn't cooperating. She'd disappeared from sight.

Morgan *was* keeping to herself, not to brood, but to work. Concentrating on her plans for her third ship, Morgan talked and corresponded with her sisters about the red tape involved in dealing with a foreign government, and she quickly found herself inundated with memos filled with valuable advice from Lisa in France and Heather in Scotland.

With Stefanie's help Morgan began making contacts among the politicians and civil servants of the Bahamas to check out the local technicalities that might create problems.

Work and family were all she needed to be content, Morgan told herself whenever images of Cole Jameson tried to nudge their way into her mind. Whatever happened, the Sinclairs could depend on each other. What else really mattered?

On a sultry, overcast evening after several days of hoping in vain to run into Morgan, Cole was restless and only one step away from despondent. Another trip to Miami was proving necessary for the sake of the island project, and he'd have to leave in the morning for perhaps as long as a week.

He couldn't stand going away without seeing Morgan first. As he wandered through the shadowy, rain-washed streets of Old Town, trying to decide whether she would welcome him if he went to her, he found himself drawn to Mallory Dock, remembering the moments he'd spent there with Morgan, recalling how lovely she'd looked with the sunset in her hair and mischief in her eyes.

He stopped dead in his tracks when he reached the dock, when he saw the moon's reflection on soft golden curls. "Morgan," he whispered, drinking in the loveliness of her slender but sweetly curved form in a filmy yellow dress, silhouetted against the charcoal sky.

Like a sleepwalker he slowly moved toward her.

Morgan was standing on the deserted dock, looking out over the water, deep in troubled thought, totally unable to shake her longing for Cole Jameson.

Suddenly a footfall behind her warned her that someone was approaching.

As a rush of adrenaline surged through her she whirled around, instantly ready to defend herself against the person creeping up on her.

Cole spoke her name a second time, loud enough for her to hear.

She was silent for a moment, still poised for action, but forcing herself to breathe evenly to relax her taut muscles and dissipate her fighting instincts.

When she'd settled down a bit—though the sight of Cole kept her pulse racing—she smiled, her subdued spirits lifted merely by the sight of him. He was clean-shaven again, his hair tousled by a breeze, his body hard and inviting in the jeans and knit shirt that showed his masculine lines to such throat-catching advantage. "Hi," she said huskily, instantly suffused by a desire she couldn't deny. "It's nice to see—"

"What are you doing here?" he interrupted, shocked by the joy he felt at unexpectedly encountering her, at the same time alarmed by her foolishness. "What the devil possessed you to wander around this area alone at night?"

"I come here by myself at night quite often,"

Morgan said, puzzled by Cole's sharp tone. "I like the solitude and the sound of the music from the dockside bars down the way, and the water lapping against the—"

"Dammit, Morgan!" Cole exploded, gripping her shoulders, tempted to give her a shaking. "I can't believe you'd put yourself in such a vulnerable position! Don't you have any idea how much trouble you could run into doing things like this? Are you so innocent of the real world that you think a woman can wander anywhere without the slightest concern about being attacked?"

"Why do you do that?" Morgan asked, bemused by Cole's outburst, not sure whether to laugh, tell him to mind his own business, or throw her arms around the impossible man and hug him for being so worried about her. She placed her palms against his chest and felt his uneven, pounding heartbeat. Surprised and moved by the evidence of his emotion, she pulled her hands away.

Cole frowned, taken aback by her question. "Why do I do what?"

"One minute you act as if there's something between us, then you back off as if you'd learned I was the Freeway Strangler, and now you're blowing up at me because you think I'm putting myself in danger. Why should you care?"

Cole had no idea how to respond, so he took refuge in what he told himself was simple common sense. "I'd be worried about anyone who didn't seem to know enough to take basic precautions. Didn't your parents teach you anything about protecting yourself?"

Morgan smiled up at him, wondering whether she should tell him how close he'd come, just a few moments ago, to taking a backflip into the water. "As a matter of fact, my parents taught me a great deal about protecting myself," she said. "That's why I can wander around certain deserted docks after dark without being afraid. But you're sweet to be concerned, Cole."

"I'm . . . sweet?" He swallowed hard, his fingers tightening around Morgan's shoulders. "I'm *sweet*? You know, Morgan, your trusting innocence is scary! No wonder you're driving me right out of my mind! I don't know what to make of a woman like you!" Before he knew what he was doing, he had folded his arms around Morgan and was kissing her possessively, his hand cupping her head, his fingers laced through the tangled silk of her hair as his mouth moved over hers, parting her lips so his tongue could delve into her sweet warmth, exploring, taking, generating a heat that threatened to consume them both.

He ended the kiss as suddenly as he had begun it, raising his head and staring down at Morgan in shock. "Where were you going from here?" he asked almost harshly, as if the question were urgent.

It took a moment for Cole's words to filter through Morgan's passion-muddled brain. Her thoughts weren't on where she was going, but on where she'd found herself at the moment. She was lost in the pleasure of Cole's intoxicating scent, his hot, minty taste. Never had she experienced anything as mind-numbing as Cole's kiss. She hadn't known such sensations were possible. Warmth was spreading throughout her body to create a heady languor, making her wish Cole would hold and touch and kiss her for eternity. "Where was I going?" she finally asked in a small, breathless voice. "'I . . . I guess I was on my way, eventually, back to my cottage."

Cole was holding on to his control by a slender thread. "I'll walk you home," he said, abruptly releasing her and placing his hand on the small of her back to guide her away from the hushed solitude, where the gentle sound of the ocean nuzzling the dock conspired with a warm breeze and Morgan's subtly tantalizing fragrance to obliterate his will.

On the way to her place Morgan tried to make conversation, but Cole was distracted, answering in monosyllables, at one point removing his hand from her back with a startled motion, like someone who had discovered that his palm was resting on the burner of a stove.

When they reached the cottage, Morgan was still shaken by Cole's searing kiss. She unlocked her door, then turned to give him a questioning look, wondering what he was going to do next. He was as unpredictable and as dangerously exciting as a tropical typhoon.

"Did you manage to send Mary-Ann home last week?" he asked.

Morgan was slow to reply. "Yes," she finally answered, pulling herself together. "Mary-Ann was glad to get on a bus the next day. I think she learned a valuable lesson. She'll think twice about leaving the safety of the nest the next time she and her folks have a disagreement."

"Thanks to you, the silly kid learned her lesson the easy way," Cole remarked, not really thinking about Mary-Ann at all but too dazed to know what else to say. He couldn't believe the way he had acted just moments earlier.

"And thanks to you, as well," Morgan reminded him. "You were kind to her. In fact, I have a feeling you're a very kind, protective man." She paused, then forged ahead. "But Cole, *I* don't need your protection. It's not what I want from you."

He said nothing at first, trying to gather his thoughts. When he'd seen Morgan at the dock, he'd been assailed by feelings more intense and primitive than he'd dreamed were in him. A very large part of his reaction had been an instinct to protect her. And now she was saying she didn't need his protection. "What *do* you want from me?" he asked, his voice thick with desire and edged with challenge.

"Why do I have to want something from you?" Morgan asked softly. "Why can't I just want . . . you? To be with you, know you, touch you . . ." She was surprised by her boldness yet couldn't help what she was saying. Smiling, she added, "And perhaps, to find out why we drive each other so crazy."

Cole was silent again, at a loss as to how to respond to such a simple but startling statement. The depth of his cynicism was suddenly clear to him as he realized how difficult it was for him to conceive of a woman's wanting him just for himself. He wasn't sure he could accept the idea. But at least Morgan had said it, and he treasured her words. He took a deep breath, remembering a mundane, annoying, inescapable reality. "I . . . I have to go away tomorrow . . ."

"For long?" Morgan asked, instantly and irrationally afraid Cole would be lost to her forever.

He shook his head. "For about a week. It's . . . business." He stopped, realizing he couldn't explain to Morgan why he was going to Miami. The damn fool project with its cloak-and-dagger secrecy, he thought with a surge of anger. There were moments when he wished he hadn't started it.

Morgan was acutely aware of the way Cole suddenly clammed up. It was his privilege to keep his activities to himself, she thought with an uncomfortable prickle of concern, but she was beginning to wonder about him. A lot of strange, unsavory things went on in Key West. She prayed he wasn't involved in any of them. "Well, I guess I'll see you around town when you get back," she said, managing to keep her tone reasonably light, refusing to let Cole see how deeply he had affected her.

Cole frowned, then shook his head, understanding the impression he'd given her. "Oh, you'll see me, all right," he said, his frown turning to a bright smile with the pleased satisfaction of a student who has just grasped the intricacies of a complex mathematical formula. "I think you misunderstood me the last time we were together and again just now. I wasn't backing off from what's happening with us. Part of me still says I should, but I can't and I won't." He paused and pushed back a lock of hair that had fallen over his forehead. "I know I've been confused—and confusing—and I'm sorry. But I want you to know I haven't been toying with your emotions deliberately, Morgan. I wouldn't."

Morgan believed him. With nothing more than his quiet assurance to go on, she implicitly believed him.

He saw her acceptance and laughed quietly. "Dammit, I wanted you to trust me, but you worry me. You *shouldn't* be so trusting, Morgan. You seem to have no self-protective instincts at all! I claim my motives are pure after the way I've treated you, and you just accept it. Why aren't you wondering if I was and *still* am toying with you, using a phony sincerity ploy? It's been done, you know."

"But you just said you're not doing it," she argued reasonably. "So if I suspected you, I'd be wrong, wouldn't I? Why is it self-protective to distrust a person?"

"Because people take advantage of you, that's why," Cole said with mock patience, as if trying to drill some sense into her head. "Because you can get hurt by trusting someone who doesn't deserve it."

Morgan nodded, weighing his argument carefully. Then she smiled. "You're right, of course. But it seems to me you can get just as hurt, perhaps more so, by *not* trusting someone who *does* deserve it." After a pause she added, "And it'll take an awful lot of evidence to persuade me that Cole Jameson doesn't deserve all the trust

I'm willing to place in him." Until she'd actually uttered the words, Morgan hadn't realized she felt so strongly about Cole. Trust had crept up on her. So had other feelings, but she pushed them aside, aware she wasn't ready to face them—and neither was Cole.

Moved, stunned, Cole had no reply to Morgan's logic. And he began to get a glimmer of who Morgan Sinclair really was. This woman was no innocent, naive lamb let loose in a world of wolves, he realized. She was aware of the risks she took when she put her faith in people, choosing to believe the best of them instead of the worst.

All at once he was awed by her emotional courage. He gazed at her, wondering if he was even half as brave.

Morgan could see that Cole was having trouble with her philosophy. He wasn't the first person to assume she was a silly girl who saw the world through a pink haze of illusion. He was merely the first to whom she'd bothered defending her position. She couldn't help wondering why she'd done it. "Have a safe journey, Cole," she murmured.

He smiled, shook his head, then unceremoniously hauled her into his arms and kissed her with all the pent-up need of the past weeks, his hand moving over her back to mold the soft length of her body to his, his hips pressing into hers as she arched herself against him. Yet somehow he still controlled himself more than Morgan could know, not allowing himself to feast on her with the slow, sweet savoring of her lips that he planned to enjoy very, very soon.

When he released her, Morgan stared at him, shaken to her depths. "The old song was off base," she said with a tremulous smile. "A kiss isn't just a kiss. With you, it's something akin to a tidal wave."

Cole chuckled with a new kind of deep, satisfying joy. "Hold that thought, Captain. When I get back to town, I'll come for you. I'll find you, whether you're at home or on your brig or in some bar with all those people who constantly surround you. And then we're going to make a new start. Agreed?"

Morgan nodded, entranced by this glimpse of the purposeful man under Cole's quiet surface. "I'll be looking forward to it," she said with a smile, then turned and hurried into the sanctity of her cottage. She tried not to dream too much about a roguish mystery man who awakened dormant needs with his strong arms and burning kisses and dark, compelling eyes.

Cole returned to Key West after four days of intense but reasonably successful negotiations with representatives from the Seminole Nation and from an Antiquities Commission he'd never heard of until it had popped up to display a surprising interest in the little archeological dig he'd financed.

He disliked the complications that seemed to be multiplying with every passing week. His aim had been to do little more than search for artifacts that might shed light on whether a fascinating account by one of his ancestors was fact or the product of a fertile imagination. Now, suddenly the project was getting out of hand.

The commuter jet touched down on the short runway of the Key West airport, and to Cole's amazement, it managed to come to an engine-whining halt before it ran out of tarmac.

As Cole sat waiting for the aisles to clear, he thought briefly about the dig itself, wondering if Dan Cypress would have any encouraging news to report. So far, the prospects had been looking bleak. Cole sometimes wondered whether he'd pin-pointed the wrong island from his ancestor's description. Yet every time he rechecked his calculations, he came up with the same spot.

Dismissing the problem, Cole smiled, realizing that now, for a little while, he could concentrate on Morgan.

After a quick trip home to shave, shower, and put on a fresh pair of slacks and a clean cotton shirt, Cole headed downtown, too late to watch the sunset, but eager to soak up the mellow atmosphere he'd missed. And most of all, to find his lady.

He checked a couple of places on Duval Street, then on a hunch headed for Captain Tony's, as if drawn by a magnet—a golden magnet with dancing eyes and ready laughter and the sweetest lips in the world.

Reaching the open doors of the bar, he went inside, stepping over a snoozing German shepherd that lay across the entrance. Cole usually visited the saloon that claimed to be the town's oldest—and looked it—earlier in the evening as a rule, and he immediately noticed a different atmosphere. The clouds of smoke were thicker, the crowd noisier, a buzz of anticipation dominating the room as the night's musicians began setting up their amplifiers and instruments.

Although Cole spotted Morgan right away, she didn't see him. She was sitting at a table beyond the far end of the bar, facing the back of the saloon. As usual she was at the eye of a human hurricane, a splash of scarlet and gold in the dim room.

Cole sat at the bar and ordered a beer, just enjoying a moment of looking at Morgan again, mulling over the possibilities for stealing her away from the crowd.

He broke into a broad grin as he realized what was going on: Cueball, sitting across from Morgan, was instructing her on the finer points of arm wrestling while she concentrated gravely on the lesson, as if arm wrestling a biker were a perfectly normal exercise for a gloriously feminine woman.

Juan was watching her, grinning like a doting father. He glanced at Cole and winked.

Sensing he'd been accepted by Morgan's unofficial protector, Cole's spirits rose, though he had no idea why Juan's opinion mattered to him.

Cole had watched the proceedings for only a few minutes when Cueball decided his pupil's arm-wrestling skills were ready for public display. "Listen, you guys," he hollered, commanding instant attention from everyone in the place. "The cap'n is real strong! I ain't kiddin'!"

"You mean she can beat you?" a high-pitched male voice a few tables away called out.

Cueball snorted derisively. "Hey, man, are you some kind of comedian?" He sounded amazed anyone would make such a ludicrous suggestion. "*Nobody* can beat me. You know that. But I've given the cap'n a few tips, so she could take you real easy, runt."

Behind Cueball, Morgan began waving her hands in the air and shaking her head, mouthing the word "No!" She couldn't help laughing at the ridiculous situation, but she felt like throttling Cueball; she hadn't expected him to turn her into a sideshow.

A small man got to his feet and approached Cueball. "What did you just call me?" he challenged bravely in his squeaky voice.

Cueball stood, hitched up his wide, studded leather belt, folded his brawny arms over his chest, narrowed his eyes, and looked down his broken nose at the small man. "I called you a runt. What do you think of that?"

Cole was worried. He'd never seen Cueball turn violent, but in Key West it didn't take much for a brawl to break out.

The little man looked Cueball up and down. "I just wanted to make sure I heard you right, that's all," he said at last, grinning lopsidedly as he added, "I'll tell you what, Cueball. I'll arm wrestle your girl. Let's see how good a teacher you are. And I warn you, I'm stronger than I look."

Cole's smile faded. He didn't like hearing Morgan referred to as Cueball's girl.

"What do you say, Cap'n?" Cueball asked her. "Do you want to put this runt in his place?"

Tension began rising within Cole. It took him a few moments to recognize that he was once again in the grip of a fierce possessiveness only Morgan had ever inspired. He didn't want the runt, Cueball, or anyone else to touch her, even in fun. The power of the emotion rocked him.

But he had nothing to say about the situation, he realized with a surge of anger at himself. He hadn't earned the right to be possessive of Morgan.

"Well?" Morgan's would-be opponent said, grinning at her as he waited for a response to his challenge.

Morgan hadn't the slightest desire to play the silly game, but she felt she had to be a good sport. "Sure, Runt," she said with a wink. "You're on."

Cole was amazed at the way the insulting nickname changed character on Morgan's lips. Runt beamed as if she'd just called him Champ. She was magic. She was wonderful.

Runt took his position in the chair opposite Morgan's. After Cueball's recitation of the rules, the match began.

Morgan put everything she had into the contest. Cole wasn't surprised. Morgan would do everything with her whole heart and soul. The thought intensified his desire; visions of how she would make love flickered through his mind.

Jealousy began to take a backseat as Cole's body and imagination responded to the sensuality of Morgan's strength, to the play of muscles under her golden skin. Even the firm set to her jaw excited him.

Morgan surprised everyone, including herself. She knew she was strong, but she hadn't expected to have a chance against even a small man. When she found herself pressing back Runt's arm, her eyes widened in disbelief. He took advantage of her brief lapse and rallied, but she found some secret reserve, gritted her teeth, and a moment later was pushing Runt's arm all the way down to the table.

A spontaneous cheer went up, and Cueball raised his arms, walking around like a champion fighter. Runt was clearly embarrassed, and Morgan blinked, amazed. Then a thought struck her. "You *let* me win!"

Cole raked his fingers through his hair in an unconscious gesture of impatience. Morgan's reaction was typical of her. Didn't she have a single mean, petty bone in that gorgeous body of hers?

Runt got to his feet, looked down at Morgan, and smiled. "No, I didn't let you win, Cap'n. You beat me fair and square." Then he grinned. "And it's the most fun I've had losing anything in my whole life." He went back to his table, accompanied by spontaneous applause, beaming with pride despite the fact that he'd lost to a woman.

Cole's frustrated territorialism returned in a rush. He could imagine how much Runt had enjoyed entwining his fingers with Morgan's, feeling her forearm on his, sitting close enough to her to breathe in her light, floral scent.

Cueball looked around the room. "Anybody else?"

Morgan groaned. She'd had enough, she decided. It was time to draw the line. "No more, please! Let me go out a winner!"

Deciding his moment had come, Cole left the bar and strode slowly past the biker to stand in front of Morgan. "I'd like to give the lady a whirl," he said, deliberately infusing his words with extra meaning as he gazed at Morgan, losing himself in the multicolored lights that flickered in her eyes.

Morgan caught her breath, her heart suddenly thudding out of control, her whole body beginning to tremble. "Cole," she whispered. Beyond that single word, she couldn't speak. She was hypnotized by the determined, sensual expression in his dark eyes, his intriguing half-smile, the electricity emanating from him. He'd said he would come for her. And he had.

Six

When Cueball began listing the rules, Cole interrupted. "Hold on a minute," he said, his gaze steady on Morgan's as he folded back his sleeve. "Let's make this contest more interesting: What do I get if I win?"

Cueball scratched his bald head. "What do you think, Cap'n?"

Morgan had begun to regain her poise, and she remembered vividly the steely strength of Cole's arms. She knew she would lose this match. "You name the stakes," she said with a tiny smile.

"That's easy," Cole said quietly. "You leave here with me—and only me—as soon as the match is over."

Morgan nodded. "You're on."

Cole lowered himself into the chair opposite her

and placed his elbow on the table, his forearm and hand extended in readiness for the match.

"Hey, hold it, you guys," Cueball said. "What does the captain get if *she* wins?"

Cole raised his brow questioningly, continuing to hold Morgan's gaze.

She didn't know what to say. But certain she'd lose the match—and win something far more interesting—she smiled as a mischievous inspiration came to her. "We're in Margaritaville, so let's play by Margaritaville Rules."

"Margaritaville Rules?" Cueball repeated, scratching his bald head. "I never heard of 'em."

Morgan wasn't surprised; she'd never heard of them either. But she spoke with conviction. "According to Margaritaville Rules, I get to name my prize *after* I win."

Cole nodded, his onyx eyes penetrating. "Fine with me, Cap'n."

"Well, then," Cueball said with a shrug, "I guess it's okay by me too."

Morgan put her elbow on the table and clasped Cole's hand. A familiar, blazing heat surged through her when his long fingers meshed with hers, and as she felt his strength, she knew that even at her best she would be no match for him; with her insides softening and her limbs melting, she didn't have a chance against him in arm wrestling or anything else.

The unfamiliar resolve in Cole's manner thrilled her. The uncompromising hardness of his body beckoned to her soft curves, made the blood pound in her head until she was dizzy. She couldn't concentrate on something as trivial as a test of strength when she was so close to Cole, when she was intoxicated by the musky male scent of him.

He was utterly beautiful, she thought as she gazed down at their entwined arms, hers slender and pale, his coppery and muscular.

Cole smiled. "Give it your best shot," he said softly. "For Runt's sake."

"Maybe Runt wore me down," Morgan suggested in an effort to pretend there was still some fight left in her. As pride made her summon every bit of power she still had, the match began.

Cole was pleased to feel her resistance. Moments later he realized his victory wasn't going to be quite as easy as he'd thought. Morgan was remarkably strong. He'd expected to have to make the contest look real by pretending she was giving him a battle, but to his amazement she caught him off guard with such a forceful attack, he had to work a little to fight his way back.

The revelation that Morgan was a worthy opponent fueled his excitement. "You've done some weight training?" he asked in a low voice.

"A little, and a bit of gymnastic work with the acrobats on my ship," Morgan answered absently, enjoying Cole's touch too much to care what form it took. Aware that a prolonged contest would keep him close to her, she was inspired to unexpected feats of strength.

"You're quite the lady," Cole said in a low voice. "Let me in on the secret. What's the prize if you win?"

Morgan smiled at him. "You'll see."

Cole loved the gleam of fun and challenge in her eyes. "Oh, I will, will I?" he said, deciding it was time to pull out all the stops. He began forcing Morgan's arm down . . . down . . .

Suddenly Cueball's huge paws came out of nowhere, curled around both opponents' hands, and flattened Cole's arm on the table under Morgan's.

When they looked quizzically at the biker, he grinned. "Margaritaville Rules. I get to help."

Cole laughed, then looked at Morgan. "You win, after all. Now I discover what prize you're going to claim."

Smiling, Morgan spoke very softly. "I take you away from here. You leave with me, and only me. Now."

Cole's pulse went wild. "You've got it, Cap'n," he said huskily, catching her hand in his, standing up and pulling her to her feet, not even trying to hide his eagerness.

A disgusted groan from the onlookers filled the room. Cole bent his head to whisper into Morgan's ear, the warmth of his breath sending new thrills through her. "I'm afraid these people are like kids at a cowboy movie. They see a mushy part coming, and they don't like it."

"I know," Morgan said, managing a laugh. "Let's make our getaway before we're pelted with popcorn."

Hand in hand they hurried out of the bar as Cueball began calling for an arm-wrestling opponent of his own, the musicians hit three twanging chords of introduction, and the tiny girl who was the bartender for the evening yelled to one of the tables, "Another round over there, you guys?"

Cole didn't slow the pace even after he and Morgan were outside. "The beginnings of a hurtin' song, the growl of a biker looking for a grudge match, and the bellow of a ninety-pound bartender are great in their place," he said as he let go of Morgan's hand and slid his arm around her waist. "But there has to be a more romantic setting for what I have in mind."

Cole waited until the shouts and car horns and ghetto blasters were far behind them, until he and Morgan had reached a tree-lined avenue so quiet he could hear the whisper of her skirt as she walked. Then he drew her toward the shelter of a giant banyan and caught her to him, his arm still around her waist, the fingertips of his free hand tracing the silken contours of her face.

Morgan rested her palms against his chest. Under his shirt she could feel his heart racing. Closing her eyes, she succumbed to the delicious sensations pervading her body.

"Do you know how long I've wanted to steal you away like this?" Cole murmured, brushing his lips over her velvety mouth.

"Since about five minutes after I first wanted you to?" she suggested softly.

They toyed with each other's lips, their kisses eager but tentative, their bodies barely touching as they surrendered to a taste of the pleasures they might share.

Cole was still taut with excitement from their

strangely sexual tussle in the bar. His lips grazed over Morgan's cheek and along her temple to her earlobe. "I'd never realized arm wrestling could be such a turn-on," he said in a low voice.

A tiny shiver of pleasure passed through Morgan as Cole's warm breath caressed her skin. "And I had no idea," she said with a catch in her voice, "what lovely things could happen under a banyan tree."

"Why are we standing here in the street?" Cole murmured, unable to let go of Morgan long enough to continue on their way.

Her eyes twinkled. "You mean we aren't in the secluded spot you mentioned?"

Smiling, Cole wondered how he could have waited so long to succumb to her allure.

With his arm around her they at last began walking again. "Nice fit," he commented after a moment, slightly surprised by how much Morgan's height appealed to him.

"What's a nice fit?" she asked, sliding her arm around his waist.

"Us," Cole answered as he drew her a little closer.

"I know." Morgan smiled up at him, deciding he was right, perhaps more than either of them realized. Her sister Heather's talk of chemistry between a man and a woman, of matches made in heaven, of soulmates searching until they found each other, suddenly didn't seem as silly as Morgan had once thought.

During their walk to his house Cole began to satisfy his curiosity about the who-when-where of

Morgan's existence. The *where* took him by surprise, even though he'd realized her background was offbeat.

"I'm from the South Pacific, strictly speaking," Morgan told him. "That's where I was born. I was raised all over the place; Mom and Dad are professional people-watchers. They're a couple of those 'ologists' who observe human behavior, trying to make sense of it: Mom's a sociologist, Dad's an anthropologist."

"Sounds like another nice fit," Cole said, squeezing his arm around her in a quick hug.

"You're right," Morgan replied, returning the hug. "They work well together, traveling all over the place."

"Which gets us back to the South Pacific, and your birth. Did the big event occur on the deck of a brigantine? Is that what led you to a life of piracy?"

"It so happens my first view of the world was from a stateroom on an ocean liner," Morgan said with a playfully defiant tilt to her chin. "I was premature. Mom was as surprised as anyone that I arrived when I did."

"Did the ship's doctor deliver you?"

"He helped. Dad handled most of the midwifery, though. Things were under control by the time the doctor showed up." Morgan smiled. "But you're not far wrong about the circumstances of my birth affecting my life. The way I grew up, sometimes spending weeks on my parents' yacht, had an even more profound influence. To this day I'm uncomfortable when I'm far from the sea." She rested her head against Cole's shoulder. "You understand what I mean, don't you? I've gotten the impression you love the ocean too."

"More than I'd realized I would," Cole answered quietly. "I also love this town, even though Conchs somehow make newcomers feel like perpetual tourists."

"They can be wary," Morgan said carefully, reluctant to hurt Cole's feelings by pointing out that he couldn't expect the locals to embrace someone who kept as much to himself as he did. She tried to broach the subject gently. "But don't forget what Juan told me about how Conchs are suspicious of privacy."

Well aware of what Morgan was driving at, Cole chose to skirt the many reasons why he was such a loner. His secret island project was only one of them. As he contrasted his habits with Morgan's ways, he realized he'd closed himself off from other people, perhaps too much. It was something to think about—another time.

For the moment he just smiled, amused by Morgan's habit of quoting Juan as the supreme Key West authority. "Your cigarmaker friend seems to be a fount of knowledge, Morgan. I've heard Juan say, however, that most Conchs are short a few palm fronds, so I can't take them too seriously. And what do you mean, *they* can be wary? I get the impression you've been accepted as a full-fledged Conch yourself."

"Impossible. A Conch is a person who was born

and raised in the Lower Keys, as I'm sure you know. According to Juan, the best I can hope for is to be considered a 'freshwater Conch.' "

"You mean, after you've lived here the seven years it reportedly takes to earn that illustrious title?" Cole asked, hoping Morgan was planning to stick around at least that long.

Morgan hesitated. She had arranged for the first mate from the New Orleans cruise to come to Key West to take the helm of the *Anne of the Indies*. A move to Nassau, at least on a temporary basis, wasn't imminent, but it wasn't far in the future. "I'm not sure what my goal is," she answered carefully. "I've always been something of a nomad, so becoming a permanent fixture anywhere is a foreign concept to me." She was quiet for another moment, then added lightly, "But in the words of the immortal James Bond, never say never."

Cole was troubled by her answer. Morgan didn't seem to be planning to leave Key West soon, but her words suggested she didn't intend to settle permanently on the island.

He was torn between cursing himself for wasting precious weeks of time he could have spent with her and reminding himself that he still wasn't sure he wanted a permanent involvement anyway.

Even in Key West, he was rapidly discovering, life could be complicated.

Cole pushed open the creaky wooden gate at his house, jarring the stillness of the evening. "Here we are," he said as his hand made a sweeping gesture toward the house that suddenly struck him as a rather ghostly looking mansion. "Welcome to the Margaritaville Mausoleum."

"It's wonderful," Morgan said with a hushed laugh. "My sister Heather would fall in love with this place. I half expect a welcoming committee of poltergeists to slither through the windows and under the doors to greet us."

"Do the Sinclair women believe in ghosts?" Cole asked, standing back to let Morgan go through the gate ahead of him.

"Only Heather, and I think she's role-playing when she weaves her tales of headless hauntings and things that go bump in the night. Heather's in Scotland, operating the otherworldly branch of Dreamweavers. Ghosts, ancient legends, fairies, magic—that's my baby sister's territory." And romance, Morgan added silently. Heather was a firm believer in the ultimate triumph of True Love. "Funny," she murmured as Cole closed the gate behind them. "You don't strike me as the white-picket-fence type."

"What type am I?" Cole asked. He almost regretted the question as soon as he'd spoken, wondering whether he really wanted to see himself through Morgan's eyes. Had she categorized him as unrealistic and irresponsible the way his family had?

Morgan glanced back at him and smiled. "You're the don't-fence-me-in type," she answered, adding, "Am I right?"

"Depends," Cole said, moving closer to her.

"On what?" Morgan asked.

"On what kind of fence it is and whether it's meant to keep me in or others out."

"You like to keep others out?"

Cole's lips twitched in a suppressed grin. "Depends."

Morgan went along with his question-and-answer game. "On what?"

"On who the others are."

She nodded. "That makes sense, I suppose."

Standing behind her, amid the lush foliage of his front yard, Cole wrapped his arms around Morgan's slim, delectably curved body, recalling the first night with her, when he'd shocked himself by holding her the same way as they'd watched the sunset. He took a deep breath, inhaling the heady scents all around him as Morgan and her sweet fragrance became part of his own special garden.

Morgan placed her hands over Cole's and leaned her head back so their cheeks were touching. She looked up at a flamboyant umbrella of flame-red blossoms in one corner of the yard. "That's one of the most beautiful trees I've ever seen," she said quietly.

"It's a royal poinciana," Cole explained, his deep voice rich with pride. "I suspect it's the real reason I bought this crazy old house that's much too big for me. I've never owned a tree before. . . ." He chuckled. "As much as a mere human can claim to own a tree. Considering the sizes and life spans of the two species, it's a bit like a gnat thinking an elephant is its house pet."

Morgan liked Cole's irreverent humor, noticing that he directed it mainly at himself. "Well, whether you own the tree or it owns you is of no consequence," she said firmly. "For the interim, you own each other. And it is a stupendous tree."

"The best part is that it's not the only tree I . . . uh . . . share space with," Cole said, pausing to kiss Morgan's temple. "Come on. I'll show you the rest of the family." He took her hand in his and led her along the narrow stone walk to the back of the house.

"Most people boast a family tree," Morgan said as she followed him. "Cole Jameson has a tree family." Her teasing stopped instantly; she gasped with delight at the exquisite hideaway created by a thick wall of greenery and bathed in the reflected aquamarine light of a small, circular pool.

"The kitchen overlooks the yard," Cole said, his voice strained with sudden emotion. He scarcely believed that Morgan was in the very setting where he'd pictured her so many times. "Would you like a drink?"

"Whatever you're having would be fine," Morgan said, too taken with her surroundings to decide.

"I'll probably have iced tea," Cole told her. "Feel free to have a cocktail, though. I don't pour with a heavy hand, and I don't believe in getting ladies tipsy so I can seduce them."

"You don't *need* to get ladies tipsy so you can seduce them," Morgan said. "Not this lady anyway."

Cole released her hand so he could stroke the nape of her neck. "You once said I couldn't seduce you. You said you'd never been seduced. I'm still not sure what you were telling me."

"Nothing very profound," Morgan answered quietly, closing her eyes and smiling with pleasure as Cole's touch sent tingles of delight coursing through her. "You seemed so worried about being a mustache-twirling villain taking advantage of a helpless female, I just felt I should remind you that I'm a big girl. I accept responsibility for what I do."

With her eyes still shut, her whole body soothed by Cole's gentle caresses, his fingers feathering over her collarbone, Morgan went on in a voice that was almost a sigh of contentment, "If we make love, it'll be because we both want to, and only because of that. It won't be because you've managed to addle my brain with your lovely kisses and caresses, or because you've made promises about tomorrow that you may or may not be able to keep."

Cole rested his hand at the top of her spine as he gazed at her for a long moment, thinking how feline Morgan was, almost purring, clearly loving to be petted, yet somehow remaining independent. He took a deep breath, slowly shook his head, then cleared his throat. "And do you want us to make love, Morgan?"

"My body wants to," she answered without hesitation. "My emotions wouldn't mind a bit. My logical mind is trailing slightly behind, however. I'd like to give it a while to catch up."

Cole chuckled and slid his arm around her shoulders to give her a tiny hug. "That suits me better than you know, Cap'n. My logical mind could use some adjusting time too. On the other hand, my body could do with some of that iced tea I mentioned. With lots and lots of ice."

As he reluctantly released Morgan and bounded up the steps to the door, taking his keys from his pocket, he heard Morgan murmur, "Good idea, Cole. Lots and lots of ice."

Seven

For hours Morgan and Cole reclined in adjacent lounge chairs, their clasped hands spanning the short distance between them, their voices muted as they shared bits of themselves in the first, tentative forays into intimacy and trust.

Part of what Cole learned about Morgan deeply disturbed him. As they talked of silly, aimless things, the conviction took root in him that she was a free spirit in a way he feared he could never be.

Even when she gazed up at the half moon that was making a sweeping arc past winking stars and wispy clouds, she spoke of her need for freedom. "Imagine doing that same revolution around the earth again and again," she mused aloud. "The identical path and direction, day after day, throughout eternity." She grinned. "If I were the moon, I'd want to try, just once, taking another trip entirely, perhaps even cutting my gravitational ties to seek my fortune out there in the great big universe."

"Think of the havoc you'd create back here on earth," Cole said, going along with her whimsy despite the uncomfortable sense that she was telling him something he ought to note well. "What would happen to the tides? How could lovers get along without the light of a silvery moon? And what would all the eccentrics in Key West do for an excuse to break loose once a month?"

Morgan laughed softly. "It does get a little strange around here when the moon's full, doesn't it?"

"It gets a little strange around this town even when the moon *isn't* full," Cole said.

"And you love the place, right?"

He nodded. "And I love the place."

"Do you miss Philadelphia?"

"Sometimes. It's where I grew up, so I'm bound to feel nostalgic about it. But what about you, Morgan? I suppose you don't have a hometown, a place that symbolizes your beginnings, a place where you can go back to see childhood friends."

"Sure I have," Morgan said with a puzzled frown. "I don't mean to sound grandiose, but really, I think of the whole world the way a lot of people think of their hometowns. I have childhood friends; they're just spread out a bit, that's all. They live in everything from huts in Kenya to high rises in Hong Kong to beach houses in California."

"It's amazing that you're so . . . so centered, I guess, though I hate resorting to that kind of jargon." Cole was genuinely curious how Morgan could seem so well-adjusted when nothing in her background seemed normal. "Most people I've met who have moved around a lot as kids feel cheated."

"I've been lucky," Morgan said, searching for a way to make Cole understand that she didn't consider herself deprived. "In fact, I often feel I've had a charmed life, seeing the world, learning about people, piling up more adventure and fun by the time I was ten than most people ever experience. You see, my parents wanted to travel. They wanted to discover things firsthand, not from books, so when they started having children, they decided to try carting us along with them. It worked out beautifully, even when they had four boisterous daughters to contend with."

"Four daughters," Cole repeated, adding a low whistle. "Quite a challenge. What about school?"

"Mom and Dad were our teachers. We took our formal education by correspondence . . . except for college, of course. Higher learning meant settling down for a while." Morgan smiled ruefully at the memory of the only difficult years she'd had in her life. "College was tough to get through, with all those boxed-in, dreary classrooms, the monotonous lectures, the same environment month after month, year after year, the same people. I felt caged."

"I know exactly what you mean." Cole vividly remembered how schoolroom walls, and later, office cubicles, had given him claustrophobia. Yet it struck him that instead of being happy to meet a woman who looked at life the same way he did, he was knocked a bit off kilter by Morgan's remarks. He'd thought of himself as a freedom-seeking rebel, but Morgan carried freedom much further than he ever had and didn't consider herself a rebel at all.

He realized that part of him was still tempted by the idea of a permanent home—or at least, a permanent home base.

Morgan didn't seem to need ties.

Cole wondered what she did need. She seemed so self-contained, so at ease in the world. He couldn't shake the unsettling thought that there was nothing he could give her that she didn't have, from material comfort to emotional security.

Swinging his long legs around until his feet hit the ground, Cole stood and tugged on Morgan's hands. "Let's sit over there," he suggested, indicating a padded wicker settee in a corner of the yard where an explosion of white, pink, and red frangipani blossoms formed a fragrant bower. "I've had enough of separate chairs."

Smiling, Morgan went with him to the settee. When she started to sit down, he calmly arranged her so she was reclining against him, her head resting on his shoulder, his arms wrapped around her. "Comfortable?" he asked, lightly kissing her forehead.

"Mmm," Morgan answered contentedly, musing that "comfortable" was hardly an adequate word. Nothing, ever, had seemed so right to her as being in Cole Jameson's arms.

"Good. By the way, I assume you don't have to

work tomorrow, or rather today. I hope I'm right, considering the hour."

"Yes, you're right. We don't run the cruise on Sundays." With sudden concern about how late it was, Morgan tried to sit up. "But I believe you have places to go on Sundays, so perhaps I should . . ." She found she couldn't move, imprisoned by the familiar strength of Cole's arms. The sensation was remarkably enjoyable.

"I don't have anything planned for this particular Sunday," he said when he'd settled her back into the crook of his arm. Idly he began tracing the outline of her mouth with his index finger, intrigued by the fullness of her lips, imagining countless pleasures they could offer. "Are you tired?" he asked.

Morgan instinctively closed her eyes, her whole body responding to Cole's subtle caress. "No, I'm not tired. But you . . ."

Cole bent his head and stilled her mouth with the lightest of kisses, then smiled at her. "I've waited for weeks for a chance to be alone with you, Captain Morgan. I have no idea how long it'll be before I get this opportunity again, given your penchant for taking on the problems of abandoned runaways, and whatever other needy characters turn to you as their last and best hope. Unless you want to leave, please don't." He kissed the tip of her nose. "There's so much more I need to learn about you."

Morgan was amazed by the way Cole's gentle kisses, strong arms, and low, husky voice could mesmerize her. But she still knew so very little about him, and the blank areas bothered her a bit. "You're sure I shouldn't go?" she asked. "You don't have to get up early to go out on your cruiser to do . . . whatever it is you do?"

"I'm sure." He gave no further explanation, deliberately—though regretfully—ignoring the cue Morgan had offered, her not-so-subtle plea for a few basic details about him. He was tempted to tell her his innocuous secret, but he'd shaken hands with Dan Cypress and everyone else involved in the excavation, vowing to keep quiet about it, and to Cole any promise was a binding trust. Besides, Morgan was a smart businesswoman. What would she think of a man who had put money into a search for artifacts of little intrinsic value, even if there was a remote—ludicrously remote—possibility of finding Spanish gold?

After an overly long silence Morgan realized that Cole simply wasn't going to talk about himself. Though she tried to respect his privacy, she couldn't help feeling that his unwillingness to open up to her marred their burgeoning closeness.

Worse, she was really beginning to worry about the reasons for his secrecy. Since the only way she knew how to deal with any problem was to get it out into the open, she decided to speak up. "Cole, do you—?" She stopped, then tried again. Even with her habit of being frank, she found it difficult to push the issue. "Do you have anything . . . well, anything sort of . . . dreadful . . . to hide?" The words sounded melodramatic and foolish even as she said them, and she waited for

Cole to laugh at her for asking such a stupid question.

It was only after a long, long moment that she realized the sickening truth: Cole wasn't coming up with a simple explanation. In fact, he wasn't saying a word.

And he definitely wasn't laughing.

He stared at Morgan, stunned by her words. "What brought that on?" He'd been playing things pretty close to the vest, but it hadn't occurred to him that Morgan would suspect him of . . . of what, he wasn't sure.

Gently extricating herself from his arms—and this time, she noticed, he let her go—she got to her feet, wandered over to the pool, and stared into its opalescent depths as she spoke carefully. "I don't want to pry, Cole. It's just that I'd hate it if you turned out to be one of the bad guys."

"What do you mean by 'bad guys'?" Cole asked evenly.

Morgan hesitated, reluctant to put her fears into words. "I guess I'm afraid I could be falling for a man who's involved in . . . well, something illicit."

"Illicit?" Cole repeated, aghast. "Like what? Like drugs from the Caribbean? Emeralds from Colombia? Guns for Central America, maybe?" Unreasonably angry, he snapped out the unpleasant possibilities before the impact of all of Morgan's words hit him fully.

Then, blinking as the rest of what she'd said registered at last, he spoke in a voice constricted by sudden emotion. "You could be falling for me?"

Morgan said nothing as she nodded almost imperceptibly. Cole found himself testing her statement. "What if I *were* one of the bad guys? Could you still fall for me?" It was a childish, crazy question, he told himself. Yet he had to hear her answer. Getting up from the settee to walk around the periphery of the garden, his hands in his pockets, his manner deceptively casual, he went on carefully. "If behind this boyish exterior there lurked a black cowboy hat and a notched gunbelt, could you still fall?"

Morgan kicked off her sandals and sat at the pool's edge, lifting her skirt to her knees as she dangled her feet in the cool water. She sat thinking about Cole's question for several moments. "I'm afraid so," she answered at last, amazed that it was true: Whatever Cole might do or be, she couldn't help the way she felt about him. "And yet, I think I'd try to catch myself before I fell any further." She sighed, moving her feet in opposite circles to create two miniature whirlpools. "It would be pretty tough, though."

Cole stopped and crouched down to examine a low clump of Chinese fan palm, though he really didn't see it at all. He couldn't seem to pull himself together, astonished that Morgan was suggesting she could care for him no matter what he was, no matter what he did. He remembered to keep the banter going while he tried to absorb the startling idea. "Who knows? Maybe you could reform me."

"I don't think so." Leaning back, her palms resting on the pool deck, Morgan looked up at the sky. "I've never believed that the love of a good woman could turn Black Bart into Blaze Glory." She smiled, finding it much easier to imagine Cole as a hero than as a villain, wishing she hadn't entertained idiotic suspicions about him. They just couldn't be true. She added with a small giggle, "The love of a good horse, maybe."

Cole circled the pool until he was behind Morgan, looking down at her. "Then I'm in trouble," he said huskily. "Because you don't look a bit like Old Paint."

"And you don't look like Black Bart," she answered softly. She tipped back her head a little farther to grin at him. "You don't look like him even when you're upside down."

Cole moved so he was beside Morgan, then dropped to a crouch as she tilted her head forward to meet his gaze. "And now?" he asked, sensing that she'd decided to offer him her trust without getting any answers from him. He thought seriously about telling her the simple truth about his project; the barrier it had caused between them was so false and unnecessary. And yet, without that barrier, he might never have known he could receive a gift as soul-restoring as Morgan's simple, unearned faith. "Do I look like Black Bart when I'm right side up?"

"What you look like," Morgan said with a twinkle of humor in her eyes, "is a sarsaparilla-drinkin', straight-shootin' rescuer of ranchers' daughters."

Cole laughed, at the same time impulsively reaching for Morgan as he decided to dispense with the foolish talk. He would explain himself enough to satisfy her curiosity later; at the moment he just wanted to slake his sudden thirst for the sweet nectar of her mouth.

He saw her eyes widen in instinctive alarm, felt her hands on his chest, and realized too late that he'd startled her with his unexpected lunge. Before he could defend himself, she'd given him a mighty shove backward. His arms flailed uselessly as he struggled to catch his balance. He landed in the pool with a resounding splash, remembering only at the last second to hold his breath. Surfacing seconds later in water up to his chest, water streaming into his eyes, he heard himself sputtering and saw Morgan on her hands and knees at the side of the pool, chewing on her lower lip and staring at him. "What was that for?" he demanded, pushing back his wet hair, wondering if he'd misread the signs she'd given him.

"I'm sorry!" Morgan said, trying to keep her voice down, trying even harder not to laugh.

Cole scowled at her. "But why did you do it?"

"I didn't mean to, Cole! It was just . . . an old habit, that's all! Blame my upbringing. My sisters. They were terrible teases, always roughhousing and pulling pranks."

"And you were the innocent angel, I suppose," Cole said. Suddenly he had to struggle to keep from chuckling. Morgan's reaction had nothing to do with whether or not she trusted him and everything to do with her instincts. And he should have anticipated her move. Hadn't she told him on the deserted dock that she could take care of herself? Of course, he hadn't paid attention. As he remembered how he'd startled Morgan that night, he knew he should be grateful he'd learned his lesson in his own pool and not in the waters off Mallory Dock.

Nevertheless he couldn't let Morgan get away with such an outrage, so he glared at her with all the menace he could summon, beckoning to her with both hands.

She glanced around behind her, as if hoping he had someone else in mind.

"You, Cap'n," Cole said with a feigned threat in his tone. "It's your turn."

Morgan's eyes widened. "My turn to go into the pool?"

"Voluntarily or otherwise, wench." Cole was half-kidding, but the idea of a moonlight swim with Morgan was tempting. "I believe in an eye for an eye, a dunking for a dunking."

"But I didn't *mean* to . . ."

Cole just kept smiling and moving toward her.

Morgan hesitated. The look of wicked determination in Cole's eyes aroused a strange excitement inside her. "Fully clothed?" she asked, her breathing suddenly labored. "Or do you expect me to . . . ?" She couldn't finish the question.

Cole kept up the game. "Let's just say I wouldn't want you to ruin your pretty red dress," he said in a lazy drawl. He stripped off his sodden shirt that had been uncomfortably plastered to his skin and tossed it to one side of the pool.

Morgan swallowed hard. Cole's chest was everything she'd dreamed it would be: hard, bronzed, inviting to the touch. She wanted to feel its unyielding muscle and sinew, rub her cheek against the dark coils of hair that glistened with drops of water, press her lips against the slight indentation at his breastbone.

"Get in here, woman," Cole said in a low voice, no longer joking as he saw the desire in Morgan's eyes.

The temptation of Cole's raw masculinity and his challenging expression were too much for Morgan. With a smile she slipped into the water, her scarlet dress billowing out around her as she moved toward Cole, her hands reaching out to him.

He caught hold of her and pulled her close. "You're nuts, you know that?" he said, smiling tenderly. "You were supposed to take off the dress. Or even to tell me to go take another flying leap. You weren't supposed to . . ." He couldn't finish, his gaze slowly taking in the wondrous sight of her.

"Have I squared things?" she asked in a small voice as the look in Cole's dark eyes did strange things to her body, creating a warmth and heaviness between her thighs, a violent pounding of her heart. "Have I paid the penance for my impulsive little shove?"

For the second time in the past few minutes, Cole felt as if he were drowning. The thin cloth of Morgan's dress was transparent. Under the surface of the water her skin gleamed pale gold through the scarlet veil, the full globes of her breasts clearly outlined, their tips thrusting enticingly against the fabric. "Not quite," he murmured, releasing her hands so he could grasp her upper arms and pull her closer. The barrier of her dress was hardly noticeable as their bodies melded together.

"It seems I was even more impulsive in offering penance than in committing my original sin," Morgan whispered as Cole's lips descended to hers. The cool water did nothing to prevent the fires bursting inside her. Cole's mouth was by turns gentle and demanding, tentative and forceful. Morgan surrendered to the hot sweetness of his kiss, her hands roaming over his hard back, her legs trembling, her hips instinctively moving against Cole's as he thrust against her.

"My logical mind is making great strides in catching up with my body," Cole murmured, gently nibbling at Morgan's lower lip until it was swollen and pink, then soothing it with his tongue. "How's yours doing?" he went on, one hand cupping her head, the other sliding slowly down her spine.

Morgan moaned raggedly as a shaft of heat tore through her. "What logical mind?" she whispered. "I have no mind at all. I only have . . . Oh, lord, I want you so much, Cole."

The blood was pounding in Cole's ears and his body was gripped by a driving need for Morgan beyond anything he'd ever felt before. He captured her mouth and parted her lips with the force of his kiss, his tongue engaging hers in an eager duel.

Morgan's fingers toyed with the hair at the nape of his neck, then crept downward to rake through the triangular pelt on his chest. Cole's heart drummed against her palms; his skin was searingly hot and his body leapt with desire at her every touch.

She felt weak yet powerful. She had a new awareness of everything around her, though nothing mattered but Cole: Cole's mouth exploring hers, Cole's hands touching and enflaming every inch of her, Cole's body tormenting her with promises of untold pleasures. He blazed kisses along her jawline to her ear, then whispered softly, his warm breath sending ripples of delight through every part of her. "What good is a mind anyway? It just confuses the issue. We want each other, Morgan. Nothing else makes any sense."

Morgan still retained a tiny grain of sanity in the midst of the erotic onslaught. "I'll never be sorry if we make love, Cole," she managed to say, arching her neck to expose her throat to Cole's hungry kisses. "But it's happening too fast for me. I'd prefer to pull back, even though I'm not sure I can. I know I can't do it alone."

Cole didn't think he could do it at all. Morgan's body didn't match her words. Her body was communicating her eager surrender, her melting desire. And it was true, he told himself: She wouldn't be sorry if they made love. He wouldn't let her be sorry.

But he was too honest to go on. He remembered his decision, and his assurance to Morgan, to give them both time to be certain of their feelings. If any promise was sacred, that one was.

With a supreme effort of will he wrapped his arms around Morgan, crushing her against him, holding her, treasuring her, forcing his body to settle down. "You're right," he said at last. "It's happening too fast."

Morgan waited until her trembling had subsided before trying to speak. "Perhaps I was wrong about what I told you last week," she said at last. "Obviously I can be seduced after all."

Cole stroked her hair and touched his lips to her temple. "No, Morgan. Not by your definition at any rate. You said we'd make love only because we wanted to, not because of addled brains or empty promises. Admittedly our brains are addled, but I've made no empty promises—nor have you—and we do want each other." He laughed as he gave her an affectionate squeeze. "What's more, if you really had insisted on getting me to pull back, and I really had pressed on, I have a feeling I'd have gone for another dive to the bottom of the pool."

"I'm sorry I did that," Morgan said, nuzzling against him.

Still struggling for self-control, Cole closed his eyes. "I'm not," he told her. "I'm not sorry at all."

Morgan felt her eyes filling with tears. "You're such a special man."

Cole didn't feel special. He felt frustrated. But he managed another chuckle. "I think I'm in big trouble, that's what I think. For some reason you bring out a side of me that's nobler than I'd thought possible. I'm not sure I'm grateful, Morgan."

She nuzzled some more, beginning to get addicted to the privilege. "I happen to think all your sides are noble, Cole Jameson, so don't go modest on me."

"Okay, Cap'n. I'm Sir Lancelot, Sir Galahad, and Sir Walter Raleigh all rolled into one. And speaking of old Sir Wally, I guess if he could toss his cape over the mud for his queen's dainty feet, I can go find my lady a robe. Do you want to come inside or wait out here?"

"I'll wait," Morgan answered. "I might as well enjoy your pool, since I'm already in it."

Cole took a deep breath, summoned the will to release her, then waded out of the pool, not daring to look back, still pummeled by conflicting emotions, wondering if he was the biggest fool in history.

Eight

Morgan stayed in the water, needing its coolness. She took off her dress to wring it out, put it beside the pool, then swam a few laps to work off a sudden surplus of energy.

When Cole returned, wearing a black velour robe and carrying a blue terry-cloth wrap for Morgan, his breath caught in his throat as he saw that she was either naked or nearly so.

He hunkered down beside the ladder on the deep side of the pool, grinned, and held up the robe, wondering why he would want to torment himself with another visual feast of her luscious body.

Noting the wicked gleam in Cole's eyes, Morgan realized he thought he could tease her a little by assaulting her modesty. But she had little physical modesty, thanks to her casual shipboard upbringing and the several trips her family had made to places where people were devoid of such self-consciousness. She decided to play Cole's game anyway, just for the fun of it. "You're not going to be a gentleman and turn your back?" she asked as she swam toward him.

"You've watched too many old movies." Cole kept his grin in place and tried to maintain a nonchalant manner despite a renewal of heat and tension within him. "No sane man would turn his back on a woman like you."

Pleased by the compliment, Morgan laughed and decided to call his bluff. She reached the ladder, curled her fingers around its handles, put one foot on the bottom rung, and lifted herself out of the water, then stopped. The game had backfired. She was paralyzed by the expression that spread over Cole's features.

Cole was transfixed, stunned into silence, his grin fading as he gazed at Morgan's slender body. Her shoulders were smoothly rounded, her breasts were high and full, her torso was a sculptor's vision of feminine perfection. A wisp of blue silk at the apex of her thighs merely enhanced the dizzying impact of her nudity. She was temptation personified, sensuality incarnate, yet she was an innocent Eve in his private Eden, ingenuous and guileless and utterly trusting. And he intended, at whatever cost, to be worthy of her trust.

His fascination became centered on one tiny drop of water that slid onto Morgan's shoulder from her hair. It meandered over her skin like a rivulet charting its course across a plain, gathered speed on its journey over the slope of her breast, reached the velvety tip, and remained poised there, suspended, as if reluctant to let go.

It was like dew on a rosebud, Cole thought, captivated. He leaned down and caught the droplet on his tongue.

Morgan gasped with the shock of sudden pleasure, her fingers tightening around the cold handles of the ladder as she tipped back her head, arched her body, and closed her eyes, almost seeing the emotional sparks that shot out from that single, minuscule spot on her swollen nipple and sizzled through her whole being.

Cole straightened up again, all at once calm as his gaze swept over the lush bounty Morgan was presenting to him in an instinctive response as old as time. He'd never felt more primitively male. Sensing that something far greater than passing pleasure was involved, he was prepared to nurture it with loving patience.

After one more lingering gaze at the softly glowing gold of Morgan's body, he curved his arm around her waist to pull her from the ladder, then set her on the soft carpet of grass and helped her into the blue robe.

Morgan opened her eyes as if coming out of a trance. She managed a smile. "Are we playing with fire, or are you as controlled as you seem to be?"

"We're playing with a conflagration," Cole answered. "And you have no idea how controlled I am." He kissed each of her eyelids. "Let's go inside. I didn't realize it until I looked at the clock, but it's after four."

Morgan was shocked. "I should go home!"

"Wearing my robe?"

"People have seen worse on the streets of Key West," Morgan said. "Perhaps I could pop my dress into a clothes dryer, though. Do you have one?"

"Yes, but I suspect that dress is the drip-dry kind. Why don't we just go into the house, hang up the dress, and catch a bit of sleep? I do have extra bedrooms, obviously, and I can give you something to use as a nightgown."

"I sleep in the—" Morgan stopped in midsentence, questioning the wisdom of finishing the thought.

Cole laughed at her worried expression. "You sleep in the nude. I should have known."

"It's just that I can't stand the way nightgowns and pajamas get all bunched up. And it seems such a weird thing to do, wearing clothes to bed."

"I couldn't agree more," Cole said, refusing to picture Morgan lying naked in bed. His control could be tested only so far. He went to pick up her dress, then returned to put his arm around her shoulders and guide her into the house. "Are you hungry?" he asked on the way through the kitchen.

Morgan shook her head. Her mind wasn't on food. "I don't think I'm going to be able to sleep in this house," she said as Cole led her up the narrow, creaking staircase.

"Why not?" Cole asked, suddenly tense, wanting Morgan to like his house and fearing she didn't. "Is it too spooky?"

"It isn't the house itself that bothers me," Morgan answered, looking around approvingly at the interior, its plain, off-white walls a starkly dramatic contrast to the rich wood trim, its hard-wood floors polished to a glowing satin finish. "I think it's a lovely house. What bothers me is that you're in it. How can I sleep when I know you're lying in a bed under the same roof, perhaps even in the next room?"

At the top of the stairs Cole indicated a room down the hall from his own. "You're more tired than you realize, Morgan. You'll sleep. I'd give odds on it."

"You sound like Stefanie." It suddenly occurred to Morgan that her sister's strange, unbreakable bond with the husband she couldn't seem to live with or be happy without was no longer so puzzling. There was a dimension to the feeling between a man and a woman that was outside the realm of common sense.

"Why do I sound like Stefanie?" Cole prompted.

Morgan came back to the present with a start as Cole opened the bedroom door. "Stefanie? Oh—because you said you'd give odds on my going to sleep. My sister does that sort of thing all the time. She'll bet on anything. If you make a remark about the fact that rain is on the way, Stefanie will make a wager on what time it'll start. She's the most pragmatic person in the world, and totally responsible, but she can't resist a silly game of chance." Morgan realized she'd lapsed into agitated chatter, as she did so often with Cole, but she couldn't help it. Being in a bedroom with him was even more unnerving than she'd expected. She found herself staring at the inviting brass bed with its cushiony blue coverlet and deep pillows.

Cole took a hanger from the closet and started putting Morgan's dress on it. "So you're a pirate queen, your sister Stefanie is an addicted gambler—"

"Oh, it isn't an addiction," Morgan interrupted, not wanting to give Cole a bad impression of Steffie. "It's more of a . . . a little quirk."

"And Heather believes in ghosts," Cole added.

Morgan was slightly taken aback. "You remember that?"

"Amazing, huh? It had to be . . . oh, I'd say several hours ago that you told me how much Heather would like my haunted house," Cole said with a teasing grin. "Hey, if that evidence of my phenomenal memory impresses you, wait'll you hear this one: The fourth Sinclair sister, Lisa, is a jazz aficionada."

Morgan's eyes widened. "I can't believe it! I didn't realize you'd even heard me say that! You can kid me all you like, but I *am* impressed. I mentioned Lisa's enthusiasm for jazz just once, as far as I can recall, the night you were at Mallory Dock with your brother."

Smiling, Cole held up the hanger. "I'll go put your dress out to dry. You climb into bed."

"Yes, sir. Will you come back and tuck me in?" Morgan asked mischievously.

Cole suppressed the flare of heat inside him. "If you'll promise to keep the blankets up to your chin, I will."

"Spoilsport."

Chuckling, Cole left the room to put Morgan's dress on a small rack he kept on the second-floor deck outside his own bedroom to air the business suits he so rarely wore nowadays.

By the time he'd returned, Morgan was asleep. She had kept her promise, he noted. Almost, anyway. Lying on her back, her curls framing her face like the halo of a naughty cherub, she'd pulled up the blankets enough to cover her breasts. Her arms were at her sides, her head tilted upward facing the window, as if to catch the morning's first rays of sunlight.

Cole felt a tug at his heart as he stood looking down at her, and another moment of confusion hit him. Morgan was as relaxed in her untroubled sleep as a child, yet her sensuality was a vibrant, tangible, overwhelming force.

He moved away before it was too late.

Back in his room he stripped off his robe and got into bed, knowing that if Morgan's sister were to bet it would take him a long while to get to sleep, she'd win hands down.

"You know, you're a great cook, Cole Jameson," Morgan said as she dug her fork enthusiastically into what was left of the Sunday brunch Cole had prepared in the kitchen and served at an old-fashioned, white wrought-iron table beside the pool.

"I'm perfectly willing to accept your flattery," he said, pouring a second cup of coffee for himself and topping off Morgan's cup. "Scrambled eggs, sausage, and toast, however, don't qualify anyone for The Chefs' Hall of Fame."

"They'd qualify me," Morgan admitted cheerfully. "I've been known to ruin prepackaged macaroni and cheese."

"The ability to ruin a prepackaged dinner has nothing to do with cooking and everything to do with proving you can't cook so you won't have to try, Morgan Sinclair." Cole grinned at her over the rim of his coffee cup. "Am I right?"

She laughed, amused that Cole had seen through her ploy so easily. "It worked too. My college roommates wouldn't let me near the kitchen."

"You didn't live in a dorm and choke down cafeteria food?"

"No, thank you! Bunking in with other kids in a big old house was bad enough. Living in a dorm would have meant the end of my college days after a week. Stefanie had been through that particular mill; she moved into a house when dorm life got to her. She warned me that I'd be better off with the independent route from the start."

"Are any of your sisters married, or does the family business demand total dedication?" Cole asked, surprising himself with the blunt question —and by the tension he felt as he awaited Morgan's reply.

Morgan reflected for a moment, then answered quietly, "Stefanie's married. But she's separated from her husband." Then, hardly missing a beat, she switched to another conversational track. "You know, you haven't told me a thing about *your* family. Not even the tree family you were boasting about last night."

Cole was amazed. He'd believed Morgan Sinclair incapable of an evasion. She certainly wasn't very good at it, he thought. "Why did you change the subject?" he asked, refusing to let her get away with it.

Morgan put down her cup and sighed deeply. "First, because I don't understand what's happening with Steffie and her husband. Second, because their marital problems aren't my confidences to share."

"And third," Cole said quietly, "their separation bothers you very much."

"Well, she's my sister. I want her to be happy. And I'm fond of her husband, so I can't think of him as a villain she's well rid of. And I find . . ." Morgan paused, then went on slowly, "I find myself wondering how any couple can make it if Steffie and T.J. can't. They seemed so right together."

Cole lapsed into silence, remembering something Doug had once said, about how his two older brothers hadn't inspired him to want to settle down, what with Cole's being divorced and Adam's living in an empty showpiece of a marriage. The odds in favor of a long-term, fulfilling relationship did seem slim, Cole thought. He had accepted that gloomy prospect after his divorce, but suddenly he didn't want to accept it. He wanted to believe happy endings were possible.

Morgan didn't like the oppressive mood that had settled over them. "Anyway, back to the main point: You're a great cook," she said too brightly.

Picking up on her desire to lighten the atmosphere, Cole smiled. "As a matter of fact, I am. And one of these days I'd like to lead you into my kitchen and teach you how pleasurable the pursuit of the culinary arts can be."

"Actually, I *should* go into your kitchen," Morgan said. "I'll take care of the cleanup detail and be on my way."

"On your way where?" Cole asked in a shocked tone. "I thought we were going to spend the day together."

Morgan's pulse leapt. "We were?"

"Didn't I ask you?"

"I don't think so, Cole."

He took her hand in his. "Then I'm asking. Would you spend today with me? We could rent bicycles and explore the island, or be lazy and drive to Smathers Beach, perhaps take a picnic along. Or we could do both, or . . . or anything you'd like."

His boyish eagerness surprised and touched Morgan. She was seeing yet another unexpected side to Cole Jameson. "I'd love to rent bikes. I'd love to have a picnic. I'd love to spend the day with you. In fact, there's nothing in the world I'd like better."

Very late that night Cole walked Morgan back to her cottage. "I'll have to be quiet," she whispered at the front door. "Georgina Lund—she'll be the *Anne*'s new captain—is staying with me. She might even decide to take over the lease when I give up the place."

Cole felt a knot form in his stomach. Morgan had mentioned during their beach picnic that she planned to inaugurate a cruise in the Bahamas, but he hadn't wanted to think about her leaving Key West, so he hadn't encouraged her to talk about the future. "I didn't realize you'd be turning over the helm so soon," he said now, his voice strained.

Sensing the tension in him, Morgan hoped it meant he was in no hurry to see her move on to Nassau. "It'll be a while yet," she told him, searching his eyes. "Georgina has to go through an extensive training period."

"I'm glad," Cole said with genuine relief. He scowled as he thought about the week Morgan was facing. "It just occurred to me that I've been thoughtless, keeping you out so late. You start your days early, and with training to do—"

"Perhaps I shouldn't have stayed out so late," Morgan interrupted, gently placing her finger on Cole's lips, "but I won't let you take the blame. You weren't holding a gun to my head. How am I going to get it through to you that I'm a big girl?"

He put his hands on her slender waist and grinned. "Only in the very nicest of places, Cap'n." Lowering his mouth to Morgan's, he was careful to restrain the impulse to kiss her with all the passion he felt. The day and evening had been beautiful—but pure torture. Desire had simmered to the boiling point the entire time, heated by every glance at Morgan, every touch they shared. "Will I see you tomorrow night?" he asked when he managed to stop brushing his lips over hers.

"I . . . I could meet you downtown," she answered, not sure whether he was making a specific date with her or asking a casual question about her plans for the evening. "Juan and the others talked last night about getting together at that new Duval Street place again tomorrow."

Cole would have preferred to pick her up at home and keep her to himself, but he didn't want her to think he was going to try to edge out all her friends. "Then I'll meet you there," he said with a smile.

All at once Morgan felt awkward. It seemed strange to say good night to Cole at her door. In fact, it seemed wrong. Somehow she thought she ought to be going home with him to sleep in his bed, in his arms, to wake up beside him.

But she'd asked for more time before taking the fateful step toward intimacy—and it would be a fateful step for her, she knew, whether or not it was as important to Cole. Much as she wanted him, her strong sense of self-preservation told her to wait. "Um . . . thanks for a wonderful day . . . I mean, weekend, I guess. Dinner was terrific. Like I said, you're a great cook. I didn't know people could make conch fritters. I thought only restaurants could."

Cole shook his head and laughed. He'd discovered very quickly that Morgan hadn't underestimated her culinary abilities: As a cook's helper, she'd turned out to be strictly ornamental. But somehow her total ineptness made her all the more endearing. "It'll probably come as some surprise to you that restaurant cooking is done by people too," he said.

Morgan giggled. "No kidding? Good heavens, imagine that! The thought hadn't even occurred to me."

With another quiet laugh Cole winked at her and said good night, then hurried away before he forgot his temporary vow not to rush her into making love.

By the time he'd arrived at the bar the next evening and was sitting talking to Juan over a beer, Cole was already plotting an excuse to spirit his lovely pirate away from all the noise and confusion.

Nevertheless, while waiting for Morgan, he decided to take advantage of the private moment with the old cigarmaker. The island excavation was beginning to show some hope of success after all, and although bits of broken pottery and a few colored-glass beads weren't much to get excited about, Cole preferred to be aware of the speculation about his activities than to pretend it wasn't going on. "Tell me, Juan," he said after buying the Cuban a beer, "why are my neighbors curious about me?"

Juan sipped his brew and studied Cole for several moments, then clamped a cheroot between his lips and lit it. A lazy curl of smoke drifted up and lost itself in the thick haze suspended just below the ceiling. "They believe you could be a treasure hunter."

Cole was stunned. He hadn't expected Juan to hit so close to the bull's-eye. Even Dan and the crew members on the project hadn't admitted yet that they held any hope of finding Spanish gold, though the thought was in the back of everyone's mind. "I hate to disappoint them," Cole said lightly, "but I'm a former stockbroker keeping in touch with the markets by computer so I can send out an investment newsletter. Pretty boring stuff, wouldn't you say?"

Juan smiled enigmatically. "We know you write that paper. Why should that work stop you from seeking treasure in more exciting ways?"

"How do you know about the newsletter?" Cole asked, frowning. When Morgan had noticed the computer setup in his den, he'd explained about the newsletter to her. He hadn't expected her to keep it a secret, but had she reported it back to Juan so soon?

Juan read his thoughts. "Morgan does not speak of you, my friend. She is not that kind of woman. She listens much more than she talks. You will learn, if you stay in Key West, how difficult it is to be as private as you seem to prefer. You do use the local post office to mail those letters, yes?"

Shaking his head and laughing, Cole returned to the matter that bothered him. "But why am I thought to be a treasure hunter? Why don't people take me for, say, a narcotics cop? Or on the other hand, suspect me of something illegal?"

Juan smiled, his narrowed eyes glittering with humor. "You mind your own business too much to be with the police, and you are too secretive to be a mere criminal."

Cole laughed again, but shifted uncomfortably in his chair. "I can't quite follow the logic."

Juan blew a series of smoke rings, then smiled at Cole. "You go out on your boat in broad daylight, and it is obvious you have been cleared by the coast guard and the DEA. You return, you leave your cruiser at the marina, and walk away from it empty-handed. You buy large amounts of unperishable food and other supplies each week and have it delivered to your boat."

"I see," Cole said, shaken by the obviousness of his movements, realizing he still had a lot to learn about small-town life. He hadn't expected his grocery orders for the crew on the island to become common knowledge. He tried a bluff. "Okay, so I'm a treasure hunter. Where are my divers? How have I marked the spot where a sunken Spanish galleon lies?"

"Now, there is an interesting question," Juan answered. "It has ended many conversations about you and your treasure. No one is sure of what you are doing because of those very puzzles. I have my own theory."

"Would you care to share it with me?" Cole asked, feigning a great deal more coolness than he felt.

"I do not believe you are searching for sunken treasure," Juan said, settling back for a long chat. "There is a very old, obscure story about how a certain tribe of Indians decided to leave Florida at the beginning of the last century," Juan said, carefully watching Cole. "They built dugouts with sails and set out from a spot near present-day Tampa, heading for the Bahamas. But they had not left the Gulf before a storm washed them ashore on a small island. I have noticed, Cole, that your daily journeys take you in the direction of certain unmarked, uninhabited islands in the Gulf."

Excitement as well as concern had began to grip Cole, but he continued pretending to be calm. "Be fair, Juan. Don't leave your story there. What happened to those people?"

"They tried to live on the island," Juan answered, his penetrating gaze fixed on Cole. "But it was too small to support them for any length of time, so they built new dugouts with sails and set out once again. They were not very lucky. Another storm hit them when they were within sight of a Bahamian out-island."

Cole felt as if time had stopped. He couldn't breathe. "And?" he asked, paralyzed with anticipation.

Juan sipped his rum and puffed at his cheroot before answering. "No one survived."

But someone did survive, Cole thought as he felt the blood draining from his face. There couldn't be two stories so much alike. "Where did you hear this tale?" he asked abruptly.

"My grandfather told it to me. He had heard it as a boy from an ancient Seminole shaman."

Cole curled his fingers around his glass to keep them from trembling and took a long drink of his beer. "If no one survived the second storm," he said when he could speak without giving away his inner turmoil, "how did the shaman hear the story?"

"Not every member of the tribe had made the journey to the Bahamas. A tiny group stayed to live out their remaining years on the Gulf island. Several more returned to the mainland to make their peace with the white man's rule."

Cole drained his glass and motioned for another beer, trying to regain his equilibrium and contain his joy. His ancestor's so-called fertile imagination had produced exactly the tale Juan had related—except that according to the journal, one person, one young Spanish-Seminole girl named Maria, had been washed up on that Bahamian out-island, adopted by a kindly English family, and later had married a visiting Yankee from Philadelphia.

It was Maria's son who'd written the journal that had started Cole on his quest, mainly for evidence of the story's accuracy, but partly for a chest of Spanish gold and jewels Maria had sworn to have seen on the island. Throughout her life she'd claimed the chest had been left buried by the Indians exactly where they'd found it. No one had believed her, dismissing her tale as the wild imaginings of a girl who'd been through terrible ordeals at sea.

If Juan's story was true, Cole thought, his heart pounding, perhaps the rest of what was in the journal was fact not fiction. Perhaps the project on the island wasn't a crazy, ill-conceived scheme.

But Cole realized that secrecy was more important than ever, so he pulled himself together and spoke lightly. "It's a poignant little anecdote, Juan, but what it has to do with treasure escapes me. Anything left on the island by those Seminoles would have very little value, except of historic interest."

Juan smiled and scratched his chin. "And there, my friend, is the point that has been puzzling me."

"Have you talked it over with your local news-hounds?" Cole asked with a forced grin.

"Only with you," Juan answered. "Treasure does not interest me."

Cole was spared the need to say more when the bartender plunked his second beer in front of him, and in the next instant Cueball wandered through the side doors of the bar. Spying Cole and Juan, the biker ambled over to them, flipped the chair next to Cole around and straddled it, leaning his arms on the back as he looked at Cole. "What's new?"

The question seemed casual enough, Cole mused. But was it? Did Cueball have his own treasure theory? Or was Cueball concerned only with Morgan, acting as another of her self-appointed guardians? "Not much," Cole answered. "Did you get your Harley fixed? I haven't seen you riding it lately, and I heard you had a problem with it."

Cueball licked his two index fingers and smoothed his bushy eyebrows. "My hawg's supposed to be ready tomorrow. It better be. I don't like being without wheels. Drives me nuts. Where's the cap'n?"

As if on cue, Cole saw Morgan swing through the Duval Street door, her dress a soft peach color almost the shade of her hair. As always, his pulse began racing, his blood heating. Morgan could stir desire in him faster and more powerfully than any woman he'd ever known.

"Hi," she said breezily, her smile deliberately encompassing all three men. She felt shy with Cole, remembering the intimacies between them, wondering whether he was thinking along the same lines, not sure how to act with him. And since he was flanked by Juan and Cueball, she couldn't sit close enough to feel the reassurance of his warmth. Instead, she sank into the chair opposite him.

"Are you tired?" Cole asked.

She nodded. "It was a hectic day. Training is always so intense. But Georgina's good, so she'll learn quickly."

Cole wasn't thrilled with that bit of information.

"I need to talk to you for a minute," Cueball said to Morgan, inclining his head to indicate an empty table nearby.

Smiling apologetically at Cole, Morgan moved to the table to listen to what the biker had to say.

Cole kept his expression impassive, but he wondered what Cueball wanted now.

A few minutes later he saw Morgan nod and grin. Then she and her bald friend vigorously shook hands.

They returned to the others. "Guess what?" Morgan said with a brilliant smile. "Cueball has agreed at last to become a pirate. He's going to start training on the *Anne* next week; won't he be wonderful?"

To Cole's amazement the biker actually blushed. "Avast, maties," he said, trying out the line for size. "The cap'n even talked me into changing my little earring for one of them big hoops. Hey, what do you guys think? You've seen Georgina Lund. I was sayin' that when she takes over the brig, she oughta call herself Cap'n Raven, what with that dark hair of hers. She's cute, and she's got a style all her own, but she's gonna have to use some gimmicks so people accept her as a substitute for the original." With the zeal of a born marketing guru, Cueball began spouting his ideas for keeping up the colorful reputation Cap'n Morgan had created for the *Anne of the Indies*.

All at once, everything fell into place for Cole. He knew without the slightest doubt that he loved Morgan. It wasn't just because of her generosity, her way of helping people by patiently showing them how to help themselves, then giving them a chance to do it. For that quality, and so many others, he admired her.

The love came from a deeper source, one he couldn't understand but wouldn't question.

And it gave him unprecedented pain to hear Cueball talk about a time when Morgan wouldn't be a part of Key West—or part of his life.

Nine

At least half a dozen people were vying for Morgan's attention after about an hour, and Cole had the strange feeling that she seemed distant from him, as if hardly aware he was there. Or was he imagining things? Was he projecting himself into the future when she would leave him—unless he could find a way to hold her?

Picking up strange vibrations from Cole, Morgan felt panic overtaking her. She'd conquered so many moments of fear in her life, she felt she should be able to battle the awful feeling that came over her when she wasn't sure what Cole was thinking or feeling.

Unaccustomed to having her emotions so tied up with another person, she was frightened by the overpowering, intense need to know that he cared for her, that the weekend they'd spent together had meant more to him than a pleasant interlude. At the same time, she scolded herself for becoming so emotional so quickly.

Unable to stop herself, she suddenly bolted. "Home time," she said, leaving her half-filled glass as she pushed back her chair and stood up. With a quick wave to everyone in general, she said her usual, "See ya," and left the bar.

Cole was shocked. Then his shock turned to anger.

Juan leaned toward him and spoke quietly. "Follow her, my friend."

Cole shook his head. "Obviously she doesn't want me to."

"Obviously she does," Juan said with a tiny smile.

"I don't play those games," Cole said fiercely.

Juan's smile broadened. "No? Then go after her."

Cole hesitated, but finally tossed a few bills onto the table, got up, and strode out of the bar.

He caught up with Morgan just as she was turning off Duval Street. Grabbing her arm, he stopped her in her tracks. " 'See ya'?" he repeated. "That's it?"

Morgan stared at him, trembling all over, wondering why it seemed so difficult to know how to behave with Cole. She'd never had that problem with anyone else. "Hi," she whispered, her throat constricted by emotion.

Seeing her stricken expression, Cole understood that Morgan wasn't playing games at all; she simply didn't know what to expect from him, or what he expected of her. He put his arms around her and spoke more gently. "You shouldn't have left by yourself, Morgan. I expected to walk you home, if nothing else. You know I only went to the damned bar to meet you."

Morgan swallowed hard. "I wasn't sure . . . I didn't want to make . . . um . . . unwarranted assumptions."

Cole laughed and buried his face in the fragrant silk of her hair. "Neither did I," he said, realizing he'd been too careful, not wanting to make his own unwarranted assumptions. "Let's avoid that problem in the future by clarifying the situation between us." Though he felt it was too soon to reveal the depth of his feelings for her, he decided he could make a start. "Until further notice from either party, you're my girl, okay? I'll walk you home. I'll pick you up there as well. We'll sit with your friends at the bar, but we'll sit together. We'll go out for dinner, take in some movies, spend Sundays being lazy together, and kiss good night. And when you're ready, sweetheart, we'll make love."

Morgan closed her eyes and nodded. "I'd like that a lot," she answered with a deep sigh.

Cole pulled her against him and held her with a fierceness that stunned them both. "What's the matter with us, Morgan? Why do we keep getting so off center?"

"It's probably my fault," Morgan said. "I've never been in—" She stopped herself just before making a declaration that was foolishly premature. "I've never felt what you make me feel," she finally said, burying her face in the warm hollow of his throat.

Cole smiled and held her for a while, oblivious to the cars and bicycles whizzing past, aware only of the sense of rightness he felt when Morgan was in his arms.

Life was good to them during the next weeks. Only a few lost souls turned to Morgan for help, and soon they all learned that Cole was equally compassionate. Both Cueball and Juan appeared to accept that Morgan was Cole's girl, and consequently the rest of her multitude of friends and acquaintances backed off just a little.

Cole began to enjoy the sessions with Morgan's buddies at the bar, discovering he liked her friends, including Cueball, whose buccaneer act was the new hit of the *Anne* cruise. "You loaned Cueball the money to repair his Harley," Cole said to Morgan over a picnic lunch at Smathers Beach on their third Sunday together. He was lying on his side, feeling the heat of the sand and sun on his body, watching Morgan give vent to her lusty appetite.

"It wasn't a loan," Morgan answered as she savored the herbed chicken Cole had made. "Lord, but you're a wonderful cook," she added with heartfelt enthusiasm. The only thing that seemed more fascinating to her than their delicious lunch was Cole's delicious body, dark and muscular and dizzyingly tempting in low-slung, very short denim cutoffs. Morgan definitely wasn't interested in Cueball's outstanding debt. "Just wonderful," she repeated, licking her lips.

For the moment Cole refused to be deterred by her flattery, or by her earthy sensuality. "What do you mean, it wasn't a loan?"

"I mean, I don't make loans to my friends. If I can spare the money they need, it's theirs. If I can't, I don't give it. But Cueball insisted he'd pay it back, and he did."

Cole laughed. "So that's why he went to work for you."

"Perhaps. But I'd been trying to talk him into it from the first minute I saw him. I knew he'd be terrific. And he really was tired of being a remittance man."

Cole had learned from Cueball himself that the biker, the black sheep of his family, had collected regular checks from his father as long as he agreed to stay away from home. "So there's another person whose dignity you've rebuilt," Cole murmured.

"Cueball's finding his dignity on his own," Morgan insisted. "But I'm glad if I did help. Even though he laughed about his family's attitude, he was hurt by it. Cueball's pretty sensitive, you know."

Cole's mouth twitched with suppressed humor. "Why, of course I knew. One look at Cueball and you can see sensitivity written 'all over him. *Literally* written all over him, in fact: Butterflies, roses, hearts, girls' names—and he's a patriot besides. Did you ever see an eagle like the one on Cueball's chest?"

Morgan giggled. "He did go a bit overboard on the body decoration, didn't he?"

"Just a bit." Cole decided to drop the subject of the biker. "Now, *your* body decoration is another matter," he said, his glance following a deliberate and leisurely path up Morgan's long, tanned legs, then over the rounded hips so sweetly emphasized by her skimpy white shorts. He perused her narrow midriff, her full breasts that made tantalizing promises to spill out of her red halter top, her soft lips, her golden, laughing eyes, her spun-silk hair.

"You make me feel naked," Morgan protested softly, not really minding the sensation at all.

Cole smiled at her, glad she'd noticed. "I can't help myself. Anyway, you yourself told me that you grew up blissfully free of the shame most kids have learned by age five, so why should you care if I make you feel naked?"

"Because you make me feel . . . *naked*," Morgan said, not sure she could explain the difference.

She didn't have to explain. Cole knew the difference. And he was looking at her in that particular way to underscore that difference. Sensing that Morgan was ready to be his lover, whether or not she'd admitted it, he wanted to create a mood that would make the step an easy one for her to take.

The almost inhuman effort he'd had to make to harness his feelings had been rewarded by an unexpected bonus: His desire had deepened to an all-pervasive, erotic energy, diffusing through him so that every part of his body, every hidden recess of his being was charged with a need to possess her, please her, fuse with her. He was like a living electromagnet, drawing Morgan into the force field around him, dissipating her resistance, dissolving her will, gradually making it one with his.

"You're doing it again," Morgan said breathlessly, her body responding to Cole's gaze with rising heat and a strange lethargy that was seeping into her limbs. "You're not looking at me; you're looking into me."

Cole smiled and picked up a piece of chicken, relenting enough to glance away for a while. But throughout the day and evening he felt the power of his inner self drawing her toward him, crackling from his body to hers, manifested in each special look, each seemingly casual touch, each innocent-sounding but meaningful word.

He knew Morgan was his. He had only to claim her. Patience became easy to manage.

It was late at night, in Cole's garden, the following Saturday, and Morgan was telling one of the stories of her childhood travels that Cole was forever coaxing out of her.

As she relaxed in a lounge chair, with Cole lying on the grass by the pool, Morgan glanced at him and suddenly saw—really saw—how the moonlight cast his strangely pagan features and strong, sculptured body into dramatic relief. Wearing only form-fitting black swim trunks, his hands clasped under his head, his eyes closed as he listened to her tale, he was a portrait of beauty and power and inviting sensuality. He was everything she could want or need.

"So what happened when the bushmen saw your father's camera?" Cole asked, opening his eyes to see why Morgan had stopped talking in the middle of her adventure.

Morgan had difficulty remembering what she'd been saying. "We . . . we expected trouble," she said at last, her gaze meeting Cole's, erotic thoughts beginning to take form in her mind.

He sat up and stared at her, captivated by the expression in her eyes, already sensing that their moment had arrived. "What kind of trouble?" he asked quietly.

"We thought they would grab the camera, perhaps smash it . . . Some people still believe you steal their souls if you take their pictures. . . ." Morgan's breath became labored, her pulse throbbed unevenly.

Smiling gently as he saw the luminous softness in Morgan's eyes, Cole extended his hand.

Morgan felt his strength pouring into her as she entwined her fingers with his, exulting in the crumbling of her defenses, no longer fearing surrender.

"Lie beside me, love," Cole said quietly, rolling over onto his side and propping himself up on one elbow.

Morgan willingly obeyed, her legs too shaky to hold her. The grass was moist and cool against her back, and though she was eager to shed her skimpy white bikini, Morgan sensed that Cole should orchestrate their lovemaking.

His gaze moved over every inch of her body, a silent statement of possession that created a fluttering sensation deep within Morgan that grew more and more insistent.

With his free hand Cole smoothed back her hair and smiled down at her, then traced the delicate curve of her cheek, his touch as light as an ocean breeze.

Morgan arched her neck as Cole's fingers feathered over her throat and shoulders, the insides of her arms, the slopes of her breasts, the cleft between them. Her lips parted as she struggled to breathe, and Cole bent his head to capture her mouth with a gentleness that made her ache inside.

She reached up to lay her palm along his firm jaw, not knowing which way she liked him better: clean-shaven, as he was at this moment, or whiskered, as he usually was when he met her after he'd been out on his boat.

Morgan still knew so little about Cole; he was an enigma to her. She didn't care. What she did know was more important than mere information.

Deftly Cole untied the strings that fastened her bikini top at the back of her neck, then the hook that held it together at the front, at the same time increasing the demands of his mouth, his tongue seeking hers, fencing, stroking, thrusting.

When Cole's palm cupped one of her breasts,

Morgan felt as if she'd been waiting forever for the warm, soothing sensations that washed over her. But soon she wanted more and began caressing Cole's arms and shoulders as she thrust herself against his hand, welcoming his ever-deeper invasion of her mouth. Still she couldn't get enough of him. She inched her fingers over his back to the nape of his neck, then traveled down his chest, discovering the textures of him, the hard planes, the taut muscles.

Finally he released her mouth and bent to swirl his tongue around her hardened nipple. Morgan gave a tiny, sharp cry of pleasure, digging her fingers into his flesh.

Cole felt again the now-familiar rush of male power as Morgan moved under his hands and lips, silently begging him to give equal attention to both breasts, to her lips again.

She was all he'd dreamed of, eager and warm, as hungry for him as he was for her. When he moved his hand downward over her body, she rose up to meet him, pressing the gentle rise of her mound against his palm, gasping and raining kisses on his shoulders and throat as his fingers undid the last strings of her bikini, then began exploring the silken secrets of her womanhood.

Morgan was on fire. Heat gathered within her while flames licked at her skin. She cried out to Cole, but he kept building the conflagration until she was consumed by a blazing need.

He had honed his patience over the past weeks; he used it now to control his own hunger until he had detonated violent explosions in Morgan. He cradled her throbbing body against him with soothing kisses and gentle caresses until he could hold back no longer.

Morgan hardly noticed when Cole managed to strip himself of the last barrier of cloth between them, but she felt the rigid heat of him pressing against her thigh, and her hand inched downward to grasp him, discovering her own power in the sudden intake of his breath.

They stroked, teased, and kissed, learning how to give ecstasy to each other. No words were exchanged and none were needed; speech would have been an intrusion.

Suddenly Cole's whole being transmitted deeper, more urgent demands, his arms going around Morgan and tightening like iron bands.

Morgan's uninhibited response sent pulsating spasms through Cole's body. A violent eruption was building inside him. But still he held on, still he stayed in control.

At last, as Cole's knowing touch made Morgan shudder with pleasure, she silently urged him over her. Her entire body was in smoldering turmoil, as if wracked with fever; she twined her arms around Cole's neck and captured his mouth with hers, luring his tongue with her own, arching her back and tightening her thighs around his hips, moving under him until he plunged into her, completing the fusion that had seemed inevitable from their first encounter.

Morgan closed her eyes and let Cole carry her as

if he were the wind and ocean, she the sailing vessel swept along on uncharted waters. His rhythm was hers, his power her strength. His thrusts deepened and quickened; Morgan caught the wave of his passion and went with it on a dizzying ride, each crest higher and wilder than the one before.

Cole began relinquishing control, soaring on an energy that swept them both upward until the final peak held them suspended for an instant of infinity, then released them to float toward a gentle cove where Cole held Morgan with a tenderness he'd never known he could feel.

Morgan's lips curved in a smile of perfect contentment as she half-slept, lulled by the protective shelter of Cole's body. After what seemed like a very short while, a bird chirped tentatively above them, as if asking whether anyone else was awake.

Morgan stirred in Cole's arms. "I think it's almost morning," she whispered, opening her eyes to a slate-blue sky framed by a circle of lightly swaying palm, banyan, and poinciana leaves.

Cole kissed her forehead. "Would you like to go inside?"

"Not really," she murmured. "It's so lovely out here."

"I don't want you to catch cold." Cole kissed the top of her head before reluctantly getting up. "Wait here. I'll get robes." He stopped halfway across the yard as a stray thought hit him. "By the way, Morgan: What happened with the bushmen and the camera?"

Morgan didn't know what he was talking about for a moment. "The what?"

Cole grinned. "That whole story wasn't a put-on, was it?"

Belatedly Morgan realized what he meant, and she laughed. "No, it wasn't."

"So what happened?"

Morgan laughed again, remembering. "They posed, mugged, and generally hammed it up, then asked Dad to be sure to send them autographed copies of the magazine that had commissioned the article he was doing."

Raking his fingers through his hair, Cole chuckled and went into the house for the robes, musing that it would be a long, long time before he would ever get enough of listening to Morgan and her tales of the strange-but-true.

In fact, he thought, it would probably take a lifetime.

Much as he hated to admit to a failure, the time came when Cole knew he had to tell Morgan about his divorce.

Seated on the wicker settee in his garden while Cole paced in front of her, Morgan stared at him. "You were married?"

He nodded. "There were no kids, which turned out to be a blessing. The divorce has been final for a couple of years, and Angela—my ex—has remarried." He took a deep breath before quietly saying the rest of it. "She didn't want children with me. She's pregnant with her new husband."

Morgan heard his deep pain. She found herself wondering about the woman Cole must have loved enough to have planned a life with. She tried to picture what the former Mrs. Cole Jameson looked like, tried in vain to fathom why Angela wouldn't want to bear Cole's children. What could have destroyed that particular happy ending? So many endings weren't happy, Morgan thought sadly. And yet, hadn't the couples started out with the highest of hopes?

Suddenly, with uncharacteristic cowardice, Morgan didn't want to know any details. "Well, now you've told me about your parents, your brothers, your friends back in Philadelphia, and about . . ." She swallowed hard. "About Angela. So I have a complete picture of your family." Talking rapidly, foolishly, Morgan was trying to keep Cole from detecting the sudden lump in her throat. "But it occurs to me that I've never met the individual members of your botanical brood. The one that looks like a store-bought Christmas tree, for instance. What's its name?"

Cole answered her question, playing for time. "Come to think of it, a store-bought Christmas tree is exactly what it looks like," he said as he picked out the one Morgan was referring to. "But it's real. It's called a Chile pine. Have you ever been to Chile?"

"For six months, when I was about twelve."

"Do you recall seeing stands of artificial evergreens?"

"I'm afraid I've never been into trees," Morgan

admitted. "In fact, to me there are just two kinds: trees you can climb and trees you can't. Nature study was never my forte."

"Nor mine," Cole admitted. "At least, not until I came to Key West. For some reason I've developed an interest in flora and fauna."

"Flora and fauna?" Morgan repeated, still trying not to think about Cole's former marriage. "Flora and fauna sound like two little kids some wicked stepmother might want to lose in the woods."

"No wonder nature study wasn't your forte," Cole said with a forced grin. "You can't resist making crazy remarks during the lesson." The conversation was stupid, he thought. Why was he letting it go on? Why didn't he just tell Morgan he knew he'd hurt her by dropping the bombshell on her? Why didn't he ask her outright why she was affected so deeply? Was he afraid she would give voice to his own fear, that if he'd messed up at love once, he could mess up again? He forced himself to steer the subject back to the mundane topic of trees. "The Chile pine," he said in carefully measured syllables, "is also known as the monkey puzzle tree. I'm inclined to give it my own nickname: The tree of matrimony."

"Oh, really? Why?" Morgan asked, trembling inside, aware that Cole was going to make her face her feelings.

"Because no one can figure out how monkeys, who insist on gravitating to its branches, can hang on without impaling themselves on its sharp needles."

Morgan gave in. "Were the needles in your marriage very sharp?" she asked quietly.

"Not especially. There shouldn't have been a marriage in the first place, that's all. Why does my divorce bother you so much?"

"Because I don't understand how marriages can fall apart, how love just . . . ends. It's awful. And there's something else: I can't believe you'd make that commitment and then back out of it, and I can't imagine any reason for a woman to give you up voluntarily. Or . . . or to resist having children with you."

It took Cole a moment to absorb her words. "Thanks for the vote of confidence," he said after a long pause. "But Angie did give me up voluntarily. Eagerly. And I don't blame her, because we just didn't have what it took."

"Did you at the beginning?"

"Not from day one. There was no magic, no sizzle. Angie told me after our divorce that she'd accepted my proposal because all her friends were getting married, and she didn't want to be left out. I didn't tell her that I went to the altar for an equally lousy reason: I'd gotten sick of the dating scene, the instant, disposable relationships. I'd thought it would be nice to get started on the American Dream: The house in the suburbs, kids . . . the whole picture. Love would grow, I'd told myself. Being married would make it happen." He got up and walked over to the edge of the yard, absently peeling loose strips of bark from a tree. "I'm not too proud of my motives."

"Do you know the name of that tree?" Morgan asked.

"It's a gumbo-limbo," Cole told her. "It's also called the tourist tree, because the bark's all red and peeling, like a tourist's sunburn."

"I think it's a Cole Jameson tree," Morgan said, rising and walking over to stand behind him, slipping her arms around his waist and resting her cheek against his back. "You have to peel away a lot of layers before you get to the heart of it."

"But do you want to?" he asked with a crooked grin. "Look at what's revealed when you strip off the outside covering. It's not a pretty sight."

"I think it is," Morgan murmured. She moved to stand in front of Cole, her arms still around his waist. "I think it's a beautiful sight."

Cole cradled her face between his two hands, aching to tell her how much he loved her, yet unable to get past the emotional roadblocks he'd set up. "Do you have any idea how sweet you are, Morgan Sinclair? Everything about you: The things you do, the things you say—the way you taste." He brushed his mouth over hers and let the caresses of his tongue tell her the rest.

Morgan's mind was emptied of all thought. When Cole kissed her, she had no room for anything but sensation. "Back to your cell, I'm afraid," Cole said when he stopped to let them both catch their breath.

Laughing, Morgan eagerly returned with him to the bedroom where, with the evening sunlight streaming through the windows, the parquet floors gleaming like burnished gold, the huge oak bed welcomed her return. She slipped between the wonderfully masculine-looking, midnight-blue sheets and unraveled a few more mysteries about Cole, about herself, and about the ways of love.

Only in the quiet aftermath, nestled again in Cole's arms, did she wonder whether she could be impervious to the scars that would be left if Cole was unable to love her as she loved him.

Because he hadn't said the words, and without them, the rest of what they'd shared—as unbelievably beautiful as it had been—was little more than an unfulfilled promise.

Ten

Apart from the nagging inner doubts Cole and Morgan shared but couldn't bring themselves to talk about, the days whizzed by with the two of them glowing with contentment.

They dined one night at a dockside restaurant under a canopy of stars that seemed so close, Morgan felt as if she could reach up and steal a handful. The table's crystal sparkled, the linens were snowy white, the candles flickered, the champagne was nestled by their table in a silver stand.

As Cole smiled at Morgan across the rim of his glass, he decided he'd been right about her from the beginning. She was an angel, and in a sensuous fall of white silk, her hair upswept, she looked more like European aristocracy than a Gulf of Mexico pirate. "So at last I get to thank you with a dinner," he murmured. "For the rescue, I mean."

But the rescue he referred to went far beyond the time his cruiser's engine had died and the *Anne of the Indies* had picked him up. With Morgan he'd discovered love for the first time, and it was like a new chance at life.

Morgan smiled at him. In a black dinner jacket, his shirt gleaming white against his dark skin, Cole was revealing yet another facet of himself to her—and she fell in love with this sophisticated stranger too.

On another evening Cole was wearing his battered hat again, along with jeans and a sweatshirt, when he picked Morgan up as her brigantine docked. He'd just returned from the island project he still hadn't told her about, and he was famished.

They headed for an unpretentious little cafe Juan had recommended. After filling up on chunks of delicious Cuban bread, Morgan barely had room for her roast pork, black beans, and yellow rice. She was disappointed. "I'd wanted bread pudding for dessert," she said. "Juan says there's nothing like it."

"And I was looking forward to indulging in Key Lime Pie. But we can come back another time," Cole said reasonably.

Morgan smiled and settled for strong coffee and didn't spoil the mood by mentioning that Captain Raven was ready to take the helm of the *Anne*, or that her trip to Nassau was coming up in her schedule with alarming speed.

Cole hadn't asked her about her future plans and spoke only of wanting, not of loving her, so she assumed he was prepared to accept her departure when the time came.

One morning, after a wonderful night in Cole's bed, she left knowing he was off to his mystery destination and went home to do some paperwork while Georgina did her first solo run on the brig.

She hadn't been inside the cottage for ten minutes when the phone rang.

It was T. J. Carriere, Stefanie's husband—her estranged husband. "Your parents have gotten themselves into a mess, darlin'," he told Morgan, obviously trying very hard to sound unworried. "They've landed in some remote Central American jail. I think I can get them out without too much trouble, but I could use some help. How about it? Can you get away?"

Morgan didn't hesitate. "I'll hire a private pilot. There's a man here who's known to be willing to go anywhere, into any situation, for a price. Have you called Stefanie?"

There was a slight pause on the other end of the line before T.J. responded. "I'd rather not. The tension between Steffie and me could get in the way of what needs to be done. You can give me whatever help I need."

Morgan didn't like the idea of leaving Stefanie in the dark about the trouble, but she saw T.J.'s point. "Is there any danger involved?" she asked briskly, already making her plans.

"Hell, I hope not," T.J. answered with feeling.

Which meant, Morgan mused with a wry smile, that there definitely could be some danger involved. "Just tell me where to meet you, and I'm on my way," she said, picking up the pencil and notepad she kept by the phone.

When she was ready to leave and had hired the pilot, Morgan took a few minutes to explain the situation to Juan, asking him to let Cole know what had happened and assure him there was no need to worry. And if three days passed without word from her, Juan was to call Stefanie.

But Morgan was careful to offer no details about where she was headed. This problem was a family matter. She didn't want Cole following her. If Steffie had to step in, she would know where to go.

When Cole returned that evening, he was brimming with excitement. He was going to have to spend every day on his island for a while, working with Dan Cypress and the crew. They seemed to be on to something with their dig after all. But he didn't have to keep the project a secret from Morgan anymore; he'd had a long talk with Dan, assuring Dan that Morgan could be trusted to keep the information to herself, and Dan had gone along with that judgment.

Not finding Morgan at home, where she'd said she would be working for the day, Cole checked several places downtown. He was surprised to find Juan alone.

Moments after speaking to Juan, Cole blindly made his way back to his empty house.

He was sick. No need to worry, Morgan had said in her message. She was racing headlong into what could be a dangerous situation, and he wasn't supposed to worry. She hadn't turned to him for help. Granted, she hadn't been able to, not knowing where to find him thanks to his infernal secrecy. But would she have gone to him if it had been possible? He had no idea. Perhaps he would never know.

So there she was, depending on some mercenary pilot to take her to an unknown spot in Central America where she would do anything it took to help her mother and father out of whatever trouble they were in.

Cole went into his dark house and sat in the kitchen nook with his face buried in his hands, his only comfort those impossible words: No need to worry.

Morgan was back in Key West within seventy-two hours, about midmorning. She went straight to Cole's house, hoping to find him there, not even taking time to change from the denims she'd traveled in.

He wasn't home.

She took a cab to the marina.

His boat was gone. Obviously, she thought, Cole was off on his secret mission again, whatever it was. And just as obviously, he'd taken to heart her message that he needn't be concerned about her. Well, she hadn't wanted him to worry. Wasn't that the reason she'd asked Juan to tell him not to?

So why was she so hurt that it was business as usual for Cole?

She went to Juan's cigar shop and pasted on a bright smile. "Hi. I'm back."

The old man looked up from his worktable and nodded with no outward show of emotion, but somehow Morgan knew he was relieved to see her.

Why couldn't she be as sure of Cole's feelings?

"You don't look happy, little one," Juan said.

Morgan realized that she was going to miss Juan when she left Key West, which would be very soon—probably within days. She would miss the way he called her little one, though she towered over him. She would miss his quiet caring, his fascinating stories of the Keys, his unwavering, protective friendship.

He rose and walked around the counter in his tiny shop and put a hand on Morgan's arm as her eyes filled with tears. "You were unable to rescue your parents?" he asked gently.

Morgan shook her head. "No, Mom and Dad are fine. Everything went like clockwork."

"Tell me everything that happened," Juan said.

"My parents led a perfectly legitimate, peaceful protest against the stripping of the rain forest by a multinational timber company," Morgan said with a heavy, distracted sigh. "An overzealous company executive paid some corrupt police official to throw them into jail. T.J. knew how to find the place, got me to distract the guard and pour a few potent drinks into him so I could get the key. We took Mom and Dad right out of that filthy cell, and then T.J. went to the company man and explained about negative publicity." She managed a tiny smile. "T.J.'s a journalist. He knows how to use the power of the press."

Suddenly Morgan couldn't blink back her tears. They began spilling down her cheeks, her bottom lip quivering uncontrollably. She was horrified by her childishness. "T.J.'s a wonderful man. you know. And he loves my sister. I had no idea that he was as upset and confused by their problems as she is. We talked for hours when we were trekking through that rain forest, and he told me he wants Stefanie back, but . . ." Morgan sniffed as her tears flowed copiously. "But . . . but he doesn't know how to approach her. It isn't that T.J. doesn't care. It's that he's caught in the bind of wondering how he should . . ." Morgan couldn't go on.

Frowning, Juan led her to a chair. "Why should such news upset you so, little one? Should you not be happy?"

"I was happy." Morgan sniffed again and gratefully accepted a box of tissues Juan handed to her. "Not only because there's hope for T.J. and Steffie, but because I came back here thinking I understood Cole better, thanks to the talk with my brother-in-law. I'd decided that Cole does care for me after all, just as T.J. loves Steffie, even if he hasn't told me. Cole, I mean. But he isn't in town. He's off somewhere . . . somewhere secret. He's not the least bit worried about me."

Juan suppressed a smile. "Cole does love you, Morgan."

She jumped to her feet and began pacing, still

carrying the box of tissues, pulling out one after another as she wept. "He's never said so."

"But he shows it, little one. In a thousand ways, all the time."

"He doesn't *say* it! He doesn't give me the words."

Mopping his brow with his sleeve, Juan sank onto the chair Morgan had vacated. "Words! Always words with women! Why are words so important to you?"

"Because they're the only way we can be sure," Morgan answered, yanking an entire wad of tissues from the box and scrunching them into a ball. "Besides, Cole knows perfectly well that I'm planning to leave Key West soon to start my operation in Nassau, and he hasn't made the slightest suggestion that he doesn't want me to go."

"Perhaps he doesn't feel he has the right," Juan pointed out. "Perhaps you've given him the idea that your business and your life of perfect freedom matter more to you than he does."

Morgan stopped in her tracks and stared at Juan. "Where would the man get a dumb idea like that?"

"From you, little one?" Juan suggested with a tiny smile. He got to his feet and went to a battle-scarred, painted wooden desk in the corner of his shop. After rifling through the contents of a drawer, Juan pulled out a creased, yellowing map and returned to the counter. "I believe you are right, Morgan. Between you and Cole, many, many words are needed. You must talk with him. Do not wait until he returns tonight. Go to him now."

"I don't know where he is," Morgan muttered as Juan spread the map out on the counter.

"I do," Juan said curtly, circling a tiny, unnamed island.

Morgan blinked, her tears beginning to dry. "How do you know?"

Juan smiled and shook his head. "I am an old Cuban Conch, little one. Have I not told you many times that I know everything that happens in Key West?" He tapped a bony finger against the spot he'd circled on the map. "Go to the man. Tell him what you feel. Tell him everything."

"What if you're wrong? What if I make a fool of myself?"

With a quiet chuckle Juan folded the map and handed it to her, then turned her around and firmly pushed her out the door. "Would it be the first time, little one?"

Even Morgan had to laugh.

Eleven

Cole sat in a folding camp chair at a desk in front of his tent, shaded by a small grove of palm trees, a pen poised in his hand over the notebook where he was cataloguing the artifacts being unearthed. His gaze was fixed on the work site fifty feet away, but his thoughts were back in Key West, his heart with Morgan. He was still numb. She'd been gone for three days and there'd been no word from her.

It killed him to have to spend his days on the island, waiting impatiently for nightfall so he could get back to town and ask Juan whether she'd returned or called.

But there was nothing Cole could do to find Morgan, or to make her come back any faster, so out of loyalty to Dan and the project, he'd decided he had to pitch in and help at this crucial time.

He noticed only vaguely that the crew had

stopped what they were doing, their heads bent over something that had been handed to Dan.

Dan straightened up, his tall body a dark silhouette against the brilliant sapphire of the sky, his forehead banded by a small, twisted scarf. He spoke quietly to the others, and as they returned to their work, he strode toward Cole.

Absently wondering what was happening, Cole waited, idly musing that Dan, a full-blooded Seminole Indian and an elder of his tribe, looked as if he'd walked out of another century despite his short hair, denim cutoffs, and tank top.

The odd thing was that at times Cole thought he looked more like Dan than like Adam or Doug. And he'd always felt he had more in common with Dan than with his own brothers. The strange sense of connectedness he'd experienced when he'd first met Dan in college had triggered Cole's memory of the family Seminole legend. Even that long ago they'd talked of checking out the island someday.

"What's up?" Cole asked when Dan lowered his lanky form into the opposite chair.

Dan's jet-black eyes gleamed with satisfaction as he placed a small object on Cole's notebook.

Cole stared for several moments, not quite taking in the significance of what was in front of him. "Is it what I think it is?" he finally asked.

"Spanish gold," Dan said quietly.

As Cole pushed back his shabby fedora and gaped in disbelief at the coin, he didn't know whether to cheer or curse. Why now? he asked himself. Why not a week sooner? A week later? But recriminations against fate were beside the point. He was angry with himself. Why hadn't he worked things out with Dan a long time ago so he could have explained the project to Morgan? If he had, she'd have known where to find him. She wouldn't be off somewhere without him to protect her. And whether or not she admitted it, she needed protection. She knew how to take care of everybody but herself.

"It's possible this coin is just a stray piece," Dan cautioned. "It could have been dropped by some Spaniard who happened onto the island, or brought here by one of the Seminoles who'd picked it up on the mainland."

"Or it could have been spilled by someone who already found the sea chest the journal talks about," Cole added.

Dan grinned and thrust out his hand. "But we do have evidence now that at least part of that story was true, so welcome to the clan, brother. It seems you have a couple of drops of Seminole blood coursing through your veins after all—along with the Spanish, the Scottish, and who knows what else."

Accepting the handshake with a forced smile, Cole got to his feet. "Let's go have a look at the site."

Dan took a step, then stopped, listening. "I hear a boat," he said after a moment, and started down to the beach, leaving the grove of palm trees that sheltered the excavation site.

Cole grabbed his binoculars and raced after Dan. At the waterfront he looked through the glasses at the approaching cabin cruiser, muttering about the bad luck of having interlopers arrive just as a major find seemed imminent.

The craft slowed as it approached the shallows and dropped anchor. Cole kept watching through the binoculars, waiting for a dinghy to be lowered over the side.

Suddenly his heart leapt into his throat. A familiar golden form appeared on deck, dressed in white shorts and a tank top. "Morgan," he whispered. He was shocked. What was she doing here?

But all at once his world seemed complete again. He didn't know or care why she'd come. The first chance he got, he was going to tell her how much he loved her. He'd had it with pussyfooting around.

Morgan bent to take off her red plastic thong sandals, tucked them into the back waistband of her shorts, then pulled on a pair of swimming goggles and adjusted them over her eyes. After standing poised on the cruiser's stern for a moment, she did a smooth, shallow dive into the water and began swimming toward shore.

Cole lowered the binoculars, staring as Morgan sliced effortlessly through the waves. "Take these," he said tersely, shoving the glasses at Dan and breaking into a run, tearing down to the beach and splashing into the water to meet her.

Morgan was enjoying her swim, but she was convinced she wouldn't find Cole on this tiny island. What would he be doing here? Juan hadn't taken time to explain that part of what he claimed to know.

She'd seen a cabin cruiser in a cove along the

shoreline, but it hadn't looked much like Cole's. What was she getting herself into?

With her goggles on, Morgan could see quite well underwater, but she was unaware she had company until she'd almost reached shore. The churned-up sand was her first warning. Then, startled by a pair of legs bearing down on her, she instinctively sprang into action. Grabbing one leg, she pulled with all her might, standing up at the same time and giving a heave. A bronzed, masculine body tumbled backward, arms flailing in all directions. From the corner of her eye Morgan spotted a second man on the beach and struck a practiced karate pose, prepared to take on as many adversaries as necessary.

But the man on shore tipped back his head and laughed uproariously, and something about him vaguely reminded Morgan of . . .

She looked down, saw a familiar battered hat floating on the rippling pools of water, then pulled off her goggles. "Cole!"

He was sputtering as he struggled to his feet. "It seems to me," he managed to say as he shook his head and wiped his eyes, "that this scene is soggily familiar."

Smoothing back her dripping hair, Morgan stared at Cole, utterly shocked. "You *are* here! Juan was right!"

He faced her, his whole body trembling as surges of anger, worry, relief, and joy vied within him. His glance swept over her and a shaft of fierce possessiveness tore through him. Morgan's white top was practically transparent, her shorts not much better. He moved to stand so he was blocking Dan's view of her, though he realized his friend was finding more humor than stimulation in the scene. "Do you have to do everything the hard way, Morgan?" Cole asked, curling his fingers around her shoulders. "You don't know these waters. Why didn't you use a dinghy to get to shore? Why would you dive in without a thought for what you could be getting into? There could be barracuda or—"

"Barracuda aren't likely to attack without provocation," Morgan said defensively. "Unless, of course, a person is foolish enough to wear something shiny that attracts them."

"Tell that to Stumpy Brown," Cole said.

Morgan scowled. "Who's Stumpy Brown?"

Cole rolled his eyes in frustration. "I made the name *up*, dammit! To illustrate a point, all right? You don't *think*, Morgan. You just plunge right in, all by yourself, never mind the potential dangers!"

"You make me sound like an impetuous idiot." Morgan's thrill at finding Cole was beginning to be overshadowed by irritation and disappointment. He certainly didn't seem pleased to see her. "There was no danger," she stated firmly. "I'm a very strong swimmer, and these waters are so clear, I could see bottom all the way."

"You didn't see *me* until the last second."

Morgan remained silent, wondering if it was necessary to point out which of them had landed flat on his back.

Cole got the message. "Oh. Well . . . still. What if . . . what if Dan had attacked you?"

"She was ready, Cole," Dan yelled through cupped hands. "She looked as if she could've handled anything I could dish out!"

"Thanks, pal! You're a big help." Cole's fingers dug into Morgan's shoulders. "What am I going to do with you? You might as well be naked."

She gave him a saccharine smile. "I didn't know I was going to be met by an unwelcoming committee."

Uttering a few colorful oaths, Cole pulled off his soaked khaki shirt and held it over Morgan's head. "Put this on. It's wet, but at least the cotton is heavy enough to cover you more decently."

"Thank you so much," Morgan said, raising her arms cooperatively. "I'll accept because I'm not an exhibitionist, but I feel compelled to remind you that I happen to consider myself quite decent, with or without benefit of clothing." She let Cole tug the shirt down, but made a face, hating the constricted feeling of squirming into wet clothes. "I notice you're allowed to go bare-chested. I've never understood that particular disparity between the sexes."

"Then you've never looked in a mirror." Cole adjusted the bottom of the shirt so it was pulled down as far as possible.

"Your chest is every bit as erotically arousing as mine," Morgan said, stubbornly clinging to her argument as her only defense against the barrage of emotions suddenly battering her. Cole's touch was still electrifying.

Cole put his hands on Morgan's shoulders again, gently this time, and gazed at her, all at once not caring about anything except that she was standing in front of him, safe and feisty and more beautiful than ever. He remembered all the times and all the ways she'd shown him how erotically arousing his chest was to her. He pulled her close and wrapped his arms around her. "Why did you go without saying where? I know you couldn't get word to me right away, and I've hated myself for that situation, but I'd have gone after you, helped you, whatever."

"It wasn't your problem, Cole," she said shakily, melting into the wonderful strength of his arms. "It was a family thing."

"Anything that's a problem for you is one for me," he told her, smoothing back her hair. "Don't you know that?"

Morgan tilted her head to capture his gaze. "How would I know it?"

Cole was paralyzed for a moment. "You have a point," he said at last, deciding this wasn't the time to tell her all the things he'd been rehearsing. "What are you doing here?" he asked instead.

"I was looking for you, Cole." She spoke in a low voice. "I wanted to tell you that . . . that no matter what you do or do not feel, I love you." She frowned, remembering something Juan had said. "And I do not consider my business or my precious freedom more important than you, if that really is what you think. But make no mistake about it, I won't pressure you like some clinging, dependent . . . female. I'll go to Nassau and never look back, if that's the way you want it." She panicked as Cole stood staring at her, saying nothing. "As a matter of fact, I'll go . . . right now!" she blurted out, trying to twist out of his arms.

Cole merely tightened his hold. "Do you think I could get in on this discussion, Captain?" With a quiet, hoarse laugh he added, "And try not to look so mutinous. You're not going anywhere, Morgan. Now that you've come to this island, you'll have to stay awhile."

"Why? Why do I have to stay awhile? You're talking in riddles, Cole! If I came here when I shouldn't have, I'll leave, that's all. And I won't mention—"

With a burst of laughter Cole swept her up in his arms and carried her toward shore. "Sorry, love," he said, grinning down at her. "I've told you already: You're not going anywhere. Not without me. For the moment, Captain Morgan is second-in-command. Guess who's first?"

Morgan didn't bother struggling. She simply glared at him. "There's only one way for me to make you put me down, and I won't do it because it involves hurting you. So I'll ask nicely, Cole. Would you be the gentleman I once thought you were and put me down?"

He smiled broadly. "Of course, my tough little lovely," he said, setting her on the sandy beach and putting his arm around her waist possessively as Dan ambled over to them.

Dan was still grinning broadly as he handed Cole his soaked hat. "I rescued this thing, though I wish someone would tell me why."

Cole scowled, amazed that he hadn't given his beloved old fedora another thought after Morgan had upended him in the water. "Thanks," he muttered. "I owe you."

Dan held out his hand to Morgan. "Dan Cypress, at your service, Cap'n."

Morgan shook hands with him, again noticing that he looked a bit like Cole, though he was darker and had rougher features. "Hi, Dan," she said, managing a smile. "Would *you* tell me what's going on?"

"Sure," he answered amiably, and started to explain the dig, its purposes, and its progress in great detail.

"Uh, Dan," Cole said with a forced smile. "I'd kind of like to explain the whole thing to my girl myself, okay?"

Dan shrugged cheerfully, heading back toward the excavation site. "Sure. I'll go look for more Spanish coins."

Morgan blinked and stared at Cole. "You backed a treasure hunt? Personally?"

He winced. "Not just a treasure hunt. We have very constructive plans for what we'll do with any artifacts that turn up. We'll build a replica of the Seminole village here, for instance. A tasteful, historically accurate destination for some of the day cruises out of the Lower Keys to visit. The *Anne* might even want to make it a stop." Cole realized he was getting ahead of himself. "Okay, I know it sounds a bit crazy, but we think it could work."

"I think it's wonderful," Morgan said quietly. "And it must have been so difficult to keep the whole thing under wraps in a place like Key West."

No recriminations, Cole thought. Morgan understood. He'd been keeping his mouth shut about his love for her, taking a chance on losing her because of some lingering scars left by his divorce? Or more accurately, by the empty marriage that had made him grateful Angie had walked out? What kind of idiot had he been? "I love you, Morgan," he said tenderly, refusing to wait another second to tell her.

Morgan's eyes filled with tears. "You love me?"

"I love you so much, so totally, I can't remember when I didn't," Cole murmured, taking her two hands in his. "I should have told you how I feel. I wanted to tell you. But I didn't know how to deal with your free-spirited ways. All the time you were worrying about pressuring me, I was afraid of pressuring you. Then there was the almost paralyzing fear that if I failed at marriage once, I'd fail again. I couldn't stand the thought of failing you. And the truth is, I have so little to offer you. Nothing like what you deserve."

"What do you mean, offer me?" she asked softly. "I don't need you to offer me anything."

"I know," Cole said with a rueful smile. "That's the point. There's nothing I can give you that you couldn't get for yourself, nothing I can do for you that you couldn't do for yourself."

"I'd take issue with that last remark," Morgan said, a glimmer of mischief in her moist, tawny eyes. She was beginning to realize that Cole had spoken of marriage a moment ago. Or had he? As usual, she wasn't sure.

Cole laughed. "Okay, maybe there are a few . . . uh . . . pleasures . . . I hope . . ."

Without warning, Morgan hurled herself against him, wrapping her arms around his neck and burying her face in the hollow of his throat. "I love you, Cole Jameson. No one else can give me what I really want, what I need: You. Just you."

Cole's arms tightened around her. "Look—I don't want us to get ahead of ourselves, but I can't resist asking: Could I give you . . . could we give each other . . . one other thing, sweetheart? Not right away but eventually?" He brushed his lips over hers. "After we've been married awhile, that is?" He failed to notice that he hadn't proposed. Not properly, at any rate.

It didn't matter. Morgan let the waves of happiness wash over her, then put her lips to Cole's ear and whispered, "I'd love a whole crew of little dark-eyed, buccaneering treasure hunters who look like you."

"And apricot-haired swashbucklers just like their mother," Cole added, closing his eyes as the realization hit him that he was holding in his arms everything that mattered most to him. "And we'll show our young pirates all the Seven Seas . . ."

Morgan smiled tenderly. "And teach them about all the flowers and trees in the garden behind their wonderful old Conch house. . . ."

"I love you, sweetheart," Cole murmured, showering kisses over her upturned face. "I love you. Forgive me if I repeat myself, but I have to make up for lost time. And hear this: From now on, you and I go into all our adventures together, including heading for Nassau to inaugurate your next cruise ship. Because, my sweet Captain Morgan, I don't intend to let you get very far out of my sight again. Strong and brave and brilliant as you are, you're not going to put me through another minute of what I just went through for three days, crazy with worry—"

Morgan interrupted the scolding with a quick kiss. "You're going to be one of those overprotective husbands, are you?"

Cole nodded. "I'm afraid so. And I'm possessive as well. You might as well know it right from the start."

Twining her arms around his neck, Morgan gazed up at him and laughed softly. "Guess what, Cole: There *is* a treasure on this island. And I believe I'm the one who's found it."

Cole was about to capture her full, sweet mouth in a kiss that would ease the ache that had been part of him for three days. His mouth was just touching hers when he heard a shout.

"Cole!" Dan hollered from just inside the grove of trees lining the beach. "Get back here on the double!"

Cole glowered at Dan, then caught something in the way his partner was motioning to him.

"Cole . . . ?" Morgan asked, picking up on the urgency in Dan's tone. Quickly she put on her plastic shoes. "It couldn't be . . . do you suppose . . . ?"

Cole caught her hand in his. They started running.

Twelve

"Are you sure you don't mind that I invited T.J. to the wedding?" Morgan anxiously asked Stefanie, afraid she'd done the wrong thing.

Her older sister pinned a white frangipani blossom to Morgan's upswept hair. "Of course I don't mind," Stefanie said, her gray eyes masked as her own smooth blond hair fell forward like the peekaboo tresses of a glamorous forties movie star. "There," she said quietly. "I think the flower is the perfect touch."

Pleased with the effect as she saw her reflection in the dressing table mirror, Morgan stood and glanced out the window, smiling when she saw Juan, his cheroot firmly in place. He was supervising Lisa, Heather, Cueball, and Dan as they finished stringing Japanese lanterns all around Cole's garden.

Cole's father and brothers, dressed in almost identical three-piece suits, were setting up lawn chairs, while his mother, beautifully gowned in Oscar de la Renta's latest, was chatting and surveying the oddly mixed gathering with a look of puzzled amusement.

"I suppose Mom and Dad are in the kitchen riding herd on the caterers," Morgan said, turning to her sister in time to catch Stefanie wiping tears from her eyes. "I'm sorry, Steffie. You're upset."

"Don't be ridiculous," Stefanie scolded, taking Morgan's dress from the guest room's antique rosewood armoire and undoing the tiny buttons down the back. "It's hard for me to believe that my tomboy sister is about to get married, that's all. And I'm a bit emotional about having the whole family together. It doesn't happen often these days. Now, come and get into your dress, and I'll do you up."

When Stefanie had finished fastening the last button, she put her hands on Morgan's shoulders and turned her around. "Dear heaven, you're so beautiful."

Morgan's eyes shone as she looked at herself in the full-length mirror beside the armoire. "Thanks for helping me pick out the dress, Steffie. It is pretty, isn't it?"

Stefanie shook her head and blinked back more tears as she surveyed the gossamer gown, an ankle-length creation of ivory silk chiffon with a scalloped lace hem, its simple yet ultrafeminine lines borrowed from Edwardian times.

"Cole thanked Mom and Dad for giving him an angel," Stefanie said with a tremulous smile, then laughed. "They weren't sure what he was talking about, never having thought of you in those terms. But everybody's going to agree with him when they see you today." With a sudden twinkle in her eyes Stefanie said, "Now, if you can just act like an angel and try not to get involved in any wrestling matches or mock swordfights or . . ."

Morgan laughed. "I'll do my best. And by the way, you look pretty smashing yourself." She didn't add that the simple but elegant dress Steffie had chosen to wear happened to be T.J.'s favorite deep rose shade.

Stefanie went to the bureau and took out a velvet box. "Cole asked me to give you this." She lifted the lid and removed a large, tear-shaped pearl pendant suspended from a string of diamonds and perfectly graduated pearls. There were, as well, tiny diamond-and-pearl earrings to match.

Morgan caught her breath as Stefanie draped the necklace on her, the pendant a perfect complement to her gown's low, square neckline. "Did you know about this bauble when you zeroed in on this dress?" Morgan asked when she'd regained her poise and was putting on the earrings.

"Cole showed it to me just after I arrived. He said it was the one set you'd admired in that treasure you crazy people dug up."

Morgan held up her left hand so the marquise-cut diamond on her third finger sparkled in the late-afternoon light that was streaming through the windows. "The pearls and this ring," she said softly. "There were more elaborate things, but I thought these pieces were so pretty. You know, I feel sad for the lady they must have been stolen from by buccaneers. I hope she doesn't mind that a pretend-pirate has them now." She sighed happily. "I didn't realize I was choosing the only items Cole would take from the treasure."

"He's donating his entire share after expenses to creating a Seminole Foundation?"

Morgan nodded. "Isn't he wonderful?"

Stefanie laughed and hugged her sister. "He's absolutely wonderful. So why don't you go down to the garden and marry him?"

Morgan's mother and father shed happy tears when she exchanged her vows with Cole. All her sisters wept, Cueball beamed as if he were the matchmaker, and Juan was spotted lighting two cheroots at once.

But Morgan was dry-eyed, smiling at Cole, bursting with happiness as she gazed into his dark eyes and found infinite, unconditional love. He squeezed her hand when they were pronounced husband and wife, then winked at the minister, who grinned, turned to Morgan, and said, "You may now kiss the groom, Cap'n."

Momentarily taken by surprise but laughing quietly along with the guests, Morgan handed her bouquet of flame-red royal poinciana blossoms to Stefanie, cradled Cole's strong, handsome face in her hands, and kissed her husband for the first time.

The slightly altered traditionalism of the day continued as the time approached for Morgan and Cole to leave for their honeymoon on his cruiser. Several single guests, including Cueball, insisted on lining up to catch Morgan's bouquet.

Laughing, she turned her back, gave the flowers a mighty heave over her shoulder, then whirled to see who would catch them. The bouquet was bounced in the air a few times like a volleyball, the good-natured battle coming down to Cueball and Georgina, his Captain Raven.

Morgan clasped her hands over her head in female triumph and laughed when the bouquet fell into Georgina's hands.

"Morgan," Cole said. "Morgan, honey, you're . . ."

It was too late. She felt herself teetering backward, about to land in the pool, dismayed that her beautiful wedding gown would be ruined. Cole reached for her, caught her by the waist, and pulled her back to safety.

The guests applauded, and Morgan twined her arms around her husband's neck. "You saved me," she murmured.

He smiled tenderly at her. "What's a husband for anyway?"

Morgan gave him a meaningful look and grinned with sensual mischief. "Let's go to the boat," she whispered, "and find out."

Don't miss Stefanie Sinclair's love story in Gail Douglas's next book

The Dreamweavers:
GAMBLING LADY
November 1989
(on sale in October 1989)

THE EDITOR'S CORNER

This month we're inaugurating a special and permanent feature that is dear to our hearts. From now on we'll spotlight one Fan of the Month at the end of the Editor's Corner. Through the years we've enjoyed and profited from your praise, your criticisms, your analyses. So have our authors. We want to share the joy of getting to know a devoted romance reader with all of you other devoted romance readers—thus, this feature. We hope you'll enjoy getting to know our first Fan of the Month, Pat Diehl.

Our space is limited this month due to the addition of our new feature, so we can give you only a few tasty tidbits about each upcoming book.

Leading off is Kay Hooper with LOVESWEPT #360, **THE GLASS SHOE**, the second in her *Once Upon a Time* series. This modern Cinderella story tells the tale of beautiful heiress Amanda Wilderman and dashing entrepreneur Ryder Foxx, who meet at a masquerade ball. Their magical romance will enchant you, and the fantasy never ends—not even when the clock strikes midnight!

Gail Douglas is back with *The Dreamweavers*: **GAMBLING LADY**, LOVESWEPT #361, also the second in a series. Captaining her Mississippi riverboat keeps Stefanie Sinclair busy, but memories of her whirlwind marriage to Cajun rogue T.J. Carriere haunt her. T.J. never understood what drove them apart after only six months, but he vows to win his wife back. Stefanie doesn't stand a chance of resisting T.J.—and neither will you!

LOVESWEPT #362, **BACK TO THE BEDROOM** by Janet Evanovich, will have you in stitches! For months David Dodd wanted to meet the mysterious woman who was always draped in a black cloak and carrying a large, odd case—and he finally gets the chance when a helicopter drops a chunk of metal through his lovely neighbor's roof and he rushes to her rescue. Katherine Finn falls head over heels for David, but as a dedicated concert musician, she can't fathom the man who seems to be drifting through life. This wonderful story is sure to strike a chord with you!

Author Fran Baker returns with another memorable romance, **KING OF THE MOUNTAIN**, LOVESWEPT #363. Fran deals with a serious subject in **KING OF THE MOUNTAIN**, and she handles it beautifully. Heroine Kitty
(continued)

Reardon carries deep emotional scars from a marriage to a man who abused her, and hero Ben Cooper wants to offer her sanctuary in his arms. But Kitty is afraid to reach out to him, to let him heal her soul. This tenderly written love story is one you won't soon forget.

Iris Johansen needs no introduction, and the title of her next LOVESWEPT, #364, **WICKED JAKE DARCY,** speaks for itself. But we're going to tantalize you anyway! Mary Harland thinks she's too innocent to enchant the notorious rake Jake Darcy, but she's literally swept off her feet by the man who is temptation in the flesh. Dangerous forces are at work, however, forcing Mary to betray Jake and begin a desperate quest. We bet your hearts are already beating in double-time in anticipation of this exciting story. Don't miss it!

From all your cards and letters, we know you all just love a bad-boy hero, and has Charlotte Hughes got one for you in **SCOUNDREL,** LOVESWEPT #365. Growing up in Peculiar, Mississippi, Blue Mitchum had been every mother's nightmare, and every daughter's fantasy. When Cassie Kennard returns to town as Cassandra D'Clair, former world-famous model, she never expects to encounter Blue Mitchum again—and certainly never guessed he'd be mayor of the town! Divorced, the mother of twin girls, Cassie wants to start a new life where she feels safe and at home, but Blue's kisses send her into a tailspin! These two people create enough heat to singe the pages. Maybe we should publish this book with a warning on its cover!

Enjoy next month's LOVESWEPTs and don't forget to keep in touch!

Sincerely,

Carolyn Nichols

Carolyn Nichols
Editor
LOVESWEPT
Bantam Books
666 Fifth Avenue
New York, NY 10103

LOVESWEPT IS PROUD
TO INTRODUCE OUR FIRST
FAN OF THE MONTH

Pat Diehl

I was speechless when Carolyn Nichols called to say she wanted me to be LOVESWEPT's first **FAN OF THE MONTH**, but I was also flattered and excited. I've read just about every LOVESWEPT ever published and have corresponded with Carolyn for many years. I own over 5,000 books, which fill two rooms in my house. LOVESWEPT books are "keepers," and I try to buy them all and even get them autographed. Sometimes I reread my favorites—I've read **LIGHTNING THAT LINGERS** by Sharon and Tom Curtis twenty-seven times! Some of my other favorite authors are Sandra Brown, Joan Elliott Pickart, Billie Green, and Mary Kay McComas, but I also enjoy reading the new authors' books.

Whenever I come across a book that particularly moves me, I buy a copy, wrap it in pretty gift paper, and give it to a senior citizen in my local hospital. I intend to will all my romance books to my granddaughter, who's now two years old. She likes to sit next to me and hold the books in her hands as if she were reading them. It's possible that there could be another **FAN OF THE MONTH** in the Diehl family in the future!

60 Minutes to a Better, More Beautiful You!

Now it's easier than ever to awaken your sensuality, stay slim forever—even make yourself irresistible. With Bantam's bestselling subliminal audio tapes, you're only 60 minutes away from a better, more beautiful you!

__	45004-2	**Slim Forever**	$8.95
__	45112-X	**Awaken Your Sensuality**	$7.95
__	45081-6	**You're Irresistible**	$7.95
__	45035-2	**Stop Smoking Forever**	$8.95
__	45130-8	**Develop Your Intuition**	$7.95
__	45022-0	**Positively Change Your Life**	$8.95
__	45154-5	**Get What You Want**	$7.95
__	45041-7	**Stress Free Forever**	$7.95
__	45106-5	**Get a Good Night's Sleep**	$7.95
__	45094-8	**Improve Your Concentration**	$7.95
__	45172-3	**Develop A Perfect Memory**	$8.95

NEW!
Handsome Book Covers Specially Designed To Fit Loveswept Books

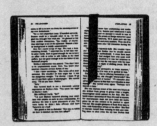

Our new French Calf Vinyl book covers come in a set of three great colors— royal blue, scarlet red and kachina green.

Each 7" × 9½" book cover has two deep vertical pockets, a handy sewn-in bookmark, and is soil and scratch resistant.

To order your set, use the form below.

Special Offer
Buy a Bantam Book
for only 50¢.

Now you can have Bantam's catalog filled with hundreds of titles plus take advantage of our unique and exciting bonus book offer. A special offer which gives you the opportunity to purchase a Bantam book for only 50¢. Here's how!

By ordering any five books at the regular price per order, you can also choose any other single book listed (up to a $5.95 value) for just 50¢. Some restrictions do apply, but for further details why not send for Bantam's catalog of titles today!

Just send us your name and address and we will send you a catalog!
